Please return/renew this item by the last date shown

OTHER BOOKS BY SALLY PRUE

Wheels of War

SALLY PRUE

OXFORD
UNIVERSITY PRESS

OXFORD

UNIVERSITY PRESS

Great Clarendon Street, Oxford OX2 6DP
Oxford University Press is a department of the University of Oxford.
It furthers the University's objective of excellence in research, scholarship,
and education by publishing worldwide in

Oxford New York

Auckland Cape Town Dar es Salaam Hong Kong Karachi
Kuala Lumpur Madrid Melbourne Mexico City Nairobi
New Delhi Shanghai Taipei Toronto

With offices in

Argentina Austria Brazil Chile Czech Republic France Greece
Guatemala Hungary Italy Japan Poland Portugal Singapore
South Korea Switzerland Thailand Turkey Ukraine Vietnam

Oxford is a registered trade mark of Oxford University Press
in the UK and in certain other countries

British Library Cataloguing in Publication Data

Data available

ISBN: 978-0-19-275439-4

1 3 5 7 9 10 8 6 4 2

Printed in Great Britain by CPI Cox & Wyman, Reading, Berkshire

Paper used in the production of this book is a natural,
recyclable product made from wood grown in sustainable forests.
The manufacturing process conforms to the environmental
regulations of the country of origin.

To Kate Williams, copyeditor extraordinaire

Chapter 1

Red, for blood. And for danger. And for soldiers, as well, bright soldiers.

Blue. That was for aloneness and sorrow.

Yellow (for gold, for joy), orange (for falling leaves, and so for glorious death), purple (for the King, far away, who can kill men with a smile).

Green, for rebellion, for hope.

Grey for ignorance. Black for death. White for sickness, the past, ghosts . . .

All of life, all of life.

Nowhere to be seen.

'I won't tell,' said Will, his heart beating fast.

George Gilfry's face was stony with distrust.

'You'll have to answer to my father,' he said. 'Perhaps to the master, even.'

Will's stomach dropped sickeningly into the darkness of his bowels. Mr Gilfry was bad enough, for he was Head Carpenter and chief of all the out-door staff, but the master . . . the master was pale, and stooped with learning, and hardly ever to be seen. He went up into the tower of the Great House every day at eight o'clock exactly to do experiments.

Will wasn't sure what an experiment was, to be truthful, but he had a vague but terrifying notion they were unnatural.

Will was going to be very alone once George had gone.

'But you will come back,' he ventured. Then, when George frowned, he went on, hurriedly, 'One day, I mean. When it's all finished. You'll come back then. Not for ages and ages, I know, because you'll be making a name for yourself, but—'

George's mouth twitched.

'In thirteen moons,' he said, faintly mocking, 'just like in the stories.'

Will caught at that.

'Yes,' he said eagerly. 'That's right. That'll be just in time for the hunters' moon, that will, and Mrs Keen will make a feast. And you shall tell us all about the places you've seen, and how many men you've killed. And you shall have a bright and shining sword, and a musket, and a fine chestnut horse, and you shall have a troop of men behind you to do just as you say.'

George grinned, and pulled the string tight round the top of his pack.

'Everyone will be abed by nine, and candles snuffed at five and twenty past,' he said. 'Now we are to keep winter hours that makes it easier for me, for there'll be no one about after that. I won't be missed until breakfast time. And then all you have to do is keep your trap shut, see?'

'Yes, George. I can do that all right.'

George ruminated a little.

'Rosie'll grieve for me,' he went on. 'She'll mope about, and weep a fair bit, I dare say.'

Will nodded regretfully. Rosie was the prettiest of the maidservants, so of course she was George's sweetheart. Will did not want Rosie to be unhappy.

'Perhaps you should tell her you're going,' he suggested. 'She'd be so proud.'

But George shook his head.

'She's a woman,' he said, dismissively. 'And women can't understand it. Going off to be a soldier, and fighting, that's stuff for men, that is.'

Stuff for men. Will's heart nearly burst with the glory of it.

'I wish I could come with you,' he said, breathlessly. 'I know I can't, sure enough, but I wish I could. Not that I'd be any trouble. I mean, I can manage without eating much. And of course I wouldn't say nothing, not if we was in company.'

George looked out through the barn window at the sunset. The fleeces that floated above the gold and scarlet trees were glowing with embers of promise.

'No,' he said, though not unkindly. 'You can't come. Being a soldier, fighting, that's the way a man takes control of his life. Makes a position for himself. You're too young, for that, yet, Will. Besides being too foolish.'

Will sighed. It was true, no army would want him, a green idiot, an orphan, cluttering up its great deeds.

'Besides,' went on George, 'they will have use for you, Will, once I'm gone.'

George hung his pack out of sight in the darkest corner of the barn. It was true that George would be badly missed. So many of the men had left to go to war that it was already a struggle to have everything about the house running to time: to have the firewood chopped, and rooms dusted, and meals served, and fires made up exactly to the minute.

Will had only ever once caught a glimpse of the master, for the master did not venture outside; but every moment of Will's life was regulated according to his rule.

'I will try to be a help to everyone,' Will said, doubtfully. 'And as for Rosie . . . well, sometimes she laughs at my foolish ways.'

George patted his shoulder.

'Good man,' he said. 'I'll rely on you to look after her for me.'

Chapter 2

'What do you mean, George isn't there?' demanded Mr Gilfry, glaring over his tankard of amber breakfast ale.

Will couldn't remember how to speak. He couldn't even remember how he usually managed to stand up, for his knees kept buckling and getting in each other's way.

'He's not in his bed, Mr Gilfry,' he blurted out.

'Well,' said Mrs Keen, the cook, comfortably, reaching across the table for the gravy jug, 'he's on his way, I expect. It's not like George to miss his breakfast, is it, Mr Gilfry.'

'That's neither here nor there,' announced Mr Gilfry, with a sharp tap on the sallow deal of the table. 'There's no place in this house for lateness, as we all well know. Will, you'd better come and sit down, now, or you'll have to be finishing before you've started.'

For the first time in his life Will didn't want to eat. When he'd first come from the almshouse he'd hardly been able to believe the amount of food on the table: pink roast meat, creamy potatoes . . . more than he could eat, there was, because he'd set out to clear up every scrap, and he'd hardly been able to believe it when he'd been defeated at last.

Mrs Keen washed down her fried onions with a genteel sip at her tankard.

'I've put a nice bit of steak aside for George, Mr Gilfry. I'll be able to fry it up quickly for him when he comes in. And with nobody any the wiser, for the mistress will be doing the accounts this morning.'

'Thank you, Mrs Keen,' said Mr Gilfry. 'But if he's not here then he must go without. He knows the master's rule.'

Will kept his trap shut as George had said, but he wished so much he could tell them: if they only knew that George had gone off to be a soldier, a bright red soldier, and when he was but fifteen years old, too. They would be so proud.

Mr Gilfry shot Will a blue glance.

'Will,' he said, quietly enough. 'Do you know what George's up to?'

Will had luckily got his mouth full of gristle. He chewed energetically and tried to forget that George had always said he was the world's worst liar. To be honest, he didn't even speak the truth all that easily.

'Well, do you, Will?'

Everyone was staring at him—Mrs Keen, and Mr Keen the butler, and two whole rows of chewing underservants. Will's tongue withered in his mouth.

Mr Keen belched slightly. 'George will have an explanation when he returns, Mr Gilfry, I'm sure. And it's not likely that the mistress will realize he's missing. Not of a Tuesday morning.'

'Well, I hope his explanation will be a good one,' said Mr Gilfry, who had been a soldier himself in his younger days and was still inclined to military severity.

People gave each other anxious sideways looks. They were all fond of George. Even Toby the garden boy, who was only really contented in the company of his spade and his dunghill, would do things if George asked him. Well, he did since George had tumbled him into the green slime of the pond, anyway.

'As long as he hasn't gone and got hisself caught in a trap,' said Mrs Keen. 'You know what these boys are like for laying snares and such like, and they're not too careful about whose land they're on. And as long as he's back for the mistress's inspection at a quarter past four.'

George would be far away by then. Miss Winter would be panic-stricken at the prospect of her brother's anger, but George would know nothing of it. Only those he'd left behind would know.

'Rosie Holmes,' said Mr Gilfry, grimly. 'Do *you* know what George is up to?'

'No, Mr Gilfry,' said Rosie, a little annoyed. 'He never said anything at all to me.'

'Hm. Well, then, we shall have to ask him about it when we see him, shan't we, you and I.'

Oh, it was a fine thing to be travelling as I pleased. The roadsides were golden with hope, and I got a lift to the camp with no trouble at all.

The soldiers were tall and strong and splendid, like gentlemen, and each had his own musket and bayonet . . . oh, they were as shining and irresistible as a band of angels.

The sergeant looked me up and down and asked my age.

And I, enraptured, lied.

It was a warm day for so far into the autumn, and the slanting golden light turned the pale stone of the house to cheese. Will forgot about George several times: but he remembered every time there were footsteps, and Mr Gilfry looked up much too quickly from his saw or his chisel.

They ate their noon-time pie outside, with the rich brown weatherboard of the barn warming their backs. 'George has a fine day for his trip,' said Mr Gilfry. 'Let's hope that the master does not look out and see him missing from his place.'

Will choked horribly on some crumbs, and Mr Gilfry looked at him speculatively, but said no more.

'George won't be here for the mistress's inspection,' said Mrs Keen, peering out of the kitchen window. 'Why, it's beginning to get dark, the evenings have drawn in so.'

Mr Blakeney shook his head. He was the master's personal servant, which meant he was as brave as a lion.

'There'll be trouble,' he said. 'The mistress will

8

have a great deal to endure over this, poor young lady. As will we all.'

'Humph. And I'll lay you'll give George something to endure, too, next time you see him, Mr Gilfry,' said Mr Keen.

Mrs Keen ran a finger between the fat folds of her pink neck and Rosie's mouth formed into a little anxious *oh!*

'I suppose,' said Mr Gilfry, brusquely, 'that he'd as soon be hanged for a sheep as a lamb.'

Toby shifted in his chair, sending a strong waft of dung round the table as he did. It permeated him. He knew it, and accepted it as an honourable part of his craft.

'You do get hanged for poaching,' he said, sorrowfully, shaking his heavy head. 'You would for taking a deer, anyway. They string you up where they caught you, they do, and bury you there, as well. I talked to a man who'd seen it done, once, and he said—'

Mrs Keen's bosom gave several powerful heaves and then she began to weep. Tears trickled from the corners of her eyes and made snail-trails through the fuzz on her rosy cheeks.

'But where can he be?' she gasped, wiping her tears away on her spotless apron and then spilling two whole gutters more. 'He has been gone all day, and he knows that the master is like to dismiss him if he steps out of his place. Where *can* he be?'

Will could not watch them suffer so. Not when he had such good, glad news. Words never came easily to him, but he grasped what courage he had.

'He's gone to be a soldier,' he blurted out: and suddenly everyone was frozen, staring at him, and all their worrying was stilled.

'He's going to fight the enemy,' he went on, more bravely, 'and he's going to get himself made officer, and find himself a fortune. And he's going to come back a gentleman, on a chestnut horse.'

He looked from one to the other of them, full of happy pride.

Mr Gilfry was the first to speak.

'How long has he been gone?' he said, and his voice grated like a dragged chair.

Will's heart beat fast with the cleverness of George's scheme.

'Since last night,' he said. 'He's been gone nearly a whole day and night, he has.'

Mrs Keen's corsets creaked with a strange moaning sound.

'You'll never catch him up,' announced Toby, lugubriously. 'He'll have got a lift up north, no trouble. He'll have taken the King's shilling by now.'

The colour had drained away from Mr Gilfry's face until it was as grey as the great bearded statue that scowled out through the leaves of the shrubbery. And then, terrifyingly, his cold eyes turned to stare at Will.

'Get out!' barked Mr Gilfry, in sudden rage. 'Get out! Go to the barn. I never want to see you again. Get out! Get out!'

The sergeant gave me a uniform. It had shining buttons and piping on the cuffs. It was not new, nor clean, but the man who had worn it had been a hero, he said.

It was too big, but then I was still growing.

Each platoon shared its rations. Mine shared with me.

I sat quiet, listening to their deep wise voices, and could have wept with pride and happiness.

Chapter 3

Will crouched, hugging his knees, flinching away from the cruel wind that spurted through the warped weatherboard of the barn walls, and he wept.

Toby stuck his head round the door a little while later, on his way to put a bit of rug over the dung heap. The amber light of his lantern moulded his heavy face into mournful folds.

'These upsets aren't good for people,' he told Will, shaking his chin. 'The mistress is all in a fright about what the master will do, and Rosie's bawling, and Mr Gilfry hardly knows which way up he is. And it all affects their digestions. You can't expect plants to flourish on the products of unhappiness, now, can you?'

It got colder and colder. Will found a bit of sacking to wrap round him. He was huddled down under the workbench, out of the worst of the wind, when someone opened the kitchen door and cast a slanted rectangle of gold into the barn.

'Will? Will?'

The door of the barn juddered a little as it scraped the frost off the cobble tops, and a silver line of moonlight traced the curve of Rosie's cheek. Will and Rosie were almost the same age, but Rosie was half a head taller than Will was, and as stout beside him as a blooming bramble to a starved pea.

'Will?' She peered into the darkness.

Will leaned forward on his numb backside until he could see the heavy hunters' moon.

'Will? Oh, there you are. You're to come in, now, Will.'

Will didn't move.

'But Mr—Mr Gilfry—' he began, his throat cluttered with cold and apprehension.

Rosie came in and squatted down before him, a busy silhouette of flaps and skirts and buttons, topped with a filmy cap.

'Mr Gilfry sent me,' she said. She spoke calmly, even kindly, but her voice was hoarse with crying. 'He says you are to come in now, Will.'

Will's joints were nearly frozen solid. He forced his legs straight and limped fearfully after her. Across the courtyard, far above him, a tall window glowed softly amber and crimson and green.

The kitchen was scented with warmth. Mrs Keen was there, and Mr Keen was sitting in his chair by the orange fire, but there was no sign of Mr Gilfry.

'Here, Will,' said Mrs Keen, kindly. 'I've heated you up a dish of broth, and never mind that it's past supper time, for we shall call it medicine. Come and get it down you.'

The broth was warm and brown and powerful: first it melted all the ice in Will's belly, and then it melted the frost in his bones. It melted and brimmed upwards and had to be wiped off on his sleeve.

'There,' said Rosie, comfortingly, as one might to a frightened child. 'Oh, but I miss him too, Will. To think that I should not see him for years, perhaps. And that I never got to say goodbye. But there. We need brave men like George to sort out these murdering rebels—'

'I'm sure it's enough to make your hair stand on end to hear the tales of them,' declared Mrs Keen.

'—and George is tall and strong. And he'll come back, I'm sure, and all fine, like you said, and with a fortune to his name, as well. So we must be brave, too.'

'You mustn't worry yourself, Will,' said Mrs Keen, stoutly. ''Twasn't your fault. We all know George: once he gets a maggot into his head there's nothing this side of hobbling that'll stop him. Even the poor mistress, she doesn't think of blaming you. And as for the master, well, he'll soon have better things to think on than Will Nunn, I'm sure. And Mr Gilfry isn't angered with you either, don't you fear. It's just that the shock made him talk sharp, that's all.'

Mr Keen gave Will a piercing look over his spectacles.

'We all know you meant well,' he said. 'But you must remember that you're just a foolish young slip of a lad, and that's why you must respect your elders and do as you're told.'

'Maybe someone will send George back,' said

Rosie, wistfully. 'Though it'd be fine if he did come back an officer, as Will said, with a scarlet coat and everything handsome about him. I'd like that full well, I would.'

The loft where Will slept was cold and empty. George's mattress lay along the wall, abandoned.

Will pulled his blanket over him and brought to mind a picture of George in a fine red coat and a tall hat. There was smoke billowing all round and explosions, but George had a shining sword in his hand and he was shouting orders to scurrying, obedient, scarlet soldiers. Rosie was standing just a little way away (though Will wasn't sure why she was there), dressed all fine like a lady, and now George was running forward to fight a green rebel soldier. Their swords clashed as they ducked and stamped and hacked. And in the end George rammed his sabre right between the rebel's ribs. And the rebel, with a look of astonishment and baffled fury, sank slowly to his knees in defeat. And there was cheering, and Rosie ran to George, and she was smiling and smiling round her. At everyone. At Will.

The vision warmed his bed as he fell asleep.

Orion is a hunter.

I watch him, from afar. He is a great friend, Orion: dependable, regular, far away. He moves according to the tables in the almanac.

But the closer ones are not so trustworthy. I discipline them, but they are weak and ignorant.

I keep them at their duties.

15

Chapter 4

They had a grey winter, a sodden spring, and a bright, emerald start to the summer. The sun coaxed them all into a bloom, soothing away their chilblains and sores and lending a sparkle of health to their eyes. Even Rufus the wagoner, who was as miserable as sin (though not half so attractive) conceded there had been worse years. There was warmth and length of days even to turn out the stuffing of the mattresses and to set the rusty hens searching through it with their black sideways eyes to pick out the bugs.

On the last Tuesday in May a troop of soldiers rode along the weedy drive and trotted thunderously under the archway into the courtyard. George was not amongst them, but they were so fine and splendidly scarlet-and-white that Will could hardly breathe for the glory of them. He stood in the dimness of the barn watching the men dismount and his heart was filled with wonder and longing.

The officer was a tall young man with a luxuriant moustache. He strode off to see the master (the *master*, who was never to be disturbed, not by anyone) and the servants gathered in an awed huddle to gawp at his men. It made quite a holiday for them, for the master did not as a rule allow strangers on his grounds.

The officer was not in the house long, so perhaps he did not get to see the master, after all. He came down escorted by the mistress, Miss Winter, who was the master's sister. Beside the officer's scarlet splendour she looked even paler and thinner and more frightened than usual. In fact she seemed too confused to take in what was happening properly, for she hardly looked at the soldiers, though most of the maids were nudging each other and whispering and giggling and making eyes at them. Why, even Rosie was looking thoughtful.

The officer clicked his heels to Miss Winter and then turned and gave an order to his sergeant.

The soldiers wore spurs, and they walked with a fine swagger so as not to trip themselves up. They made their way up to the crowd of servants, who were at first awe-struck, and then gleeful; but then, as the dreadful realization of what was happening dawned on them, they cried out with dismay and then with disbelief at their absolute powerlessness.

The soldiers took nearly all the men. Took them right away, to be soldiers. Mr Gilfry was too stiff with arthritis to go, and Toby was so busy turning over one of his dung-heaps that he was never discovered, but they took the others. All of them. They took Rufus, and Jack, and Giles, and James, and Mr Blakeney. They even took Mr Keen.

Will couldn't believe it. Just couldn't believe it. To think that Mr Keen, the great Mr Keen, the head of all the servants, should be obliged to leave them, even though Mrs Keen was crying as loud as a cow whose calf was being taken away. And there was Pamela, holding on to Giles as if she would drown without him and saying *don't go, don't go, oh don't go*; and now the soldiers were leading Jack away, too, even though Betty and Mary were bawling and red-faced and ugly with tears. And now Mr Blakeney was being led into line: white as lard, he was, and *he* was brave enough to wait upon the master, even.

They took the horses, too; even Miss Winter's blue roan pony. Young Sam, Rosie's brother, who had only been working at the house a few weeks, shamed himself by crying bitterly into Rosie's bosom. Only the two farm horses, which by chance were up in the High Field out of the way, were left behind.

They left Will behind, too. They took one look at his foolish, hopeful face and let him be, even though these past few months he'd been shooting up like a beanstalk.

The soldiers rode away, so smart and splendid and scarlet and white and black; and the men who had lived in the house walked in file amongst them. Marched, they did, in step, left-right, to the orders of a man with a chevron on his scarlet tunic. Even Mr Keen, generally so stately and dignified, marched.

Shoulders . . . BACK! Left. Left. Left-right-left.

They marched under the archway and off to— where?

Will's heart thumped with longing and envy and humiliation and terrified relief.

And then the men had gone, completely gone: and those left behind them milled around in the courtyard heart-torn and tearful, but still too bewildered to understand properly that the pattern of their lives had been ripped to shreds—still somehow hoping to be kissed and comforted and led back to where they had belonged.

But their places had vanished all along with their husbands, or lovers, or hopes-for-the-future; all gone to the wars, beyond any knowledge, or certainty of return.

Miss Winter herself seemed quite as dazed as any of them. She walked round in circles, stumbling a little, directionless, pale.

But the world was still turning round them. The great clock that ticked above the stable door began grating and clinking and rattling, and the gilded minute hand began to tremble with effort.

And then, it struck the hour.

Chapter 5

The sound of the clock shook everyone into action. The maids picked up their skirts and ran for the kitchen door, and Mr Gilfry, putting on a surprising turn of speed, just beat Will into the darkness of the barn. In a few seconds the courtyard was empty but for the lonely, horror-struck figure of Miss Winter.

But none of them could escape altogether. In a few moments Miss Winter's silhouette appeared in the barn doorway, all skirts and trembling and narrow wrists.

'William! William Nunn!'

Will shrank down as much as he could, but still he could not make himself invisible. Miss Winter took two more hurried steps into the barn and spotted him.

'We must be quick,' she said breathlessly. 'As quick as we can. The hour has struck and the master's fire has not been made up.'

The master? Will's heart turned to ice. He looked beseechingly at Mr Gilfry.

'Will's only young, ma'am,' said Mr Gilfry, 'and perhaps a bit simple. He's never been further into the house than the kitchen before. The master's never set eyes on him.'

'I know, I know, but that can't be helped. It is past the hour and my brother . . . my brother will be very much disturbed.'

Miss Winter turned to Will and he saw that her fear was as great as his own.

'It will only get worse,' she said. 'Hurry!'

And she hastened out of the barn.

Will shambled reluctantly across the courtyard after Miss Winter's anxious figure.

He had never set foot in the family's part of the house. He ate in the kitchen, he worked in the barn, he slept in the loft, and he washed, if he washed at all, in the trough by the kitchen door.

Miss Winter grasped the heavy handle of the main house door with both hands and turned it until it clicked and swung away . . .

. . . and there, there right at Will's feet, was another land. There were glowing flowers, and a high snowy sky, and a black mountain that twisted . . .

Will shook himself back into reality. The mountain was just a staircase, of course it was, of aged oak, carved all the way up in pinnacles. Thousands of hours of work, that must have been, and just on a staircase. And look, the ceiling! Moulded leaves and shields and little angels, even, with only a wisp of scarf to keep their modesty. And look there at the chest—and there—and . . .

Will, dizzy, stepped gingerly over the doormat and onto the stone flags that ran down on either side of the licheny rug.

'Come along, William,' whispered Miss Winter, her face near as pale as her hair. 'It is five past the hour. My brother will be so angry.'

The bannisters were worn with centuries of use. Will went up softly. It was like a wood that had been frozen by magic. There were leaves and vines that wound along, and sometimes amongst them was a secret mouse, or a stoat, or a little bird caught in the act of stealing a berry.

And then, as Will reached the turn of the stairs, suddenly, suddenly, the whole world changed again: the walls bloomed from chalky white to gold and green, with gouts of red like shadowed blood, and long gashes of acid-green. Will gasped in fear and amazement. Even his hands had been changed: some magic had stained them red and black and . . .

'Hurry. Do *hurry*!'

Will glanced up—and found himself looking into paradise.

Will had seen the tender shoots of spring, and summer's crimson roses, but never, ever, anything so marvellous as this. It stopped his breath.

A thin silhouette swooped down towards him over the bannister and he fell back into his skin with a jolt.

'Quickly, William,' said Miss Winter, almost pleadingly. 'Quickly.'

Will blinked, and looked again, and found not

paradise, but a window. It was made of coloured glass fitted together with strips of lead to make a picture of a soldier—but not a scarlet-and-white one like those that had come that afternoon, but one dressed all in shining armour.

'This way!'

Will tore his eyes away from the window and pushed himself up the last few stairs. Miss Winter was pattering hurriedly along the black oak boards of a landing which led each way into musty gloom. Will stumbled along behind her, even though a hundred objects—pictures, plates, chairs—were clamouring around him and taking away what wits he had.

Miss Winter stopped before a tapestry of dismal sages and mauves that hung on the wall.

'My brother—the master—does not welcome interruption,' she said, breathlessly, anxiously. 'He must never have his train of thought disturbed. So you must go in quietly, see to the fire, and then try to get out without his noticing you. Perhaps, just perhaps, he will not have noticed that the routine of the day has been disrupted. But he will be so discomposed when he discovers what has happened. So angry. But of course I could not have prevented it, and he will realize that, in time. When he becomes calmer. You'll find the logs stacked ready, William. But you must make no noise, do you understand?'

She pulled aside the tapestry. There was an oak door behind it, as narrow as a coffin's lid.

Behind it, a bone white stairway twisted upwards into darkness.

Will forced his legs to climb the stairs to the tower room. He went as slowly as he dared, but still he could not help but reach the top.

Here, where not even the shadow of a shadow could make its way round the turning stairs, all was blackness. Will felt in front of him and found a cold ring. He waited for a dozen rapid heartbeats: but nothing but the world's end could save him.

He twisted the ring and it swung away from him with barely a click.

The chamber inside was unlike anything Will had ever imagined. The house downstairs had been marvellous, but this room was wrapped in secrets.

Will gazed, open-mouthed, hardly able to believe there were so many books in all the world. His fingers itched to pull out one of the brown volumes on the shelves that lined the walls, to feel the leather binding, to let it fall open in his hands.

And what would it say? He couldn't read, of course, but he would surely be able to imbibe some of the mystery from the cream paper that would rustle so enticingly under his fingers. Yes, he was almost sure of it. The shapes of the letters would whisper something of the secrets they held.

What sort of secrets would they be, that it could not be told out loud? Things so extraordinary that speaking them might shake the plaster from the walls . . . Secrets that might make your eyes bulge and your hair stand on end so it got caught up in that twisty lamp, that was so smothered in silvery dust and spiders' webs.

What was that satinwood tray on the desk for? And the slim silver knife? Was it for an experiment? And what about that leather-bound tube that was clamped to that beech tripod?

'Who is that? Who is it? Who is there?'

The voice lashed out of nowhere, and Will's heart jolted painfully. The shadows in the corner beyond the desk were twitching, and now they were deepening and detaching themselves. *'Who is that?'*

The master was a small man, even thinner than his sister. He approached Will, as white-faced as a ghoul and as hunched as a beetle; and his inky eyes were full of rage.

'You are not the right one!'

Will would have run away, but his legs wouldn't move. No part of him would move. He couldn't even close his mouth, or breathe.

The master limped closer, blinking, each snap of the eyelids like a springing trap.

'Where is the proper man?' he demanded, shrilly. 'Speak!'

Will tried, though the first sounds that came out were too strangled to mean anything.

'He's—he's gone, sir.'

'Gone?'

'To the war, sir. Some soldiers came and took him. He's gone to fight for His Majesty.'

The master limped closer. His coat was black, and shiny with age, and he breathed as though his narrow nose could not take in enough air.

'But I have nothing to do with His Majesty,' he

snapped, suddenly, viciously. 'I have nothing to do with fighting. I am a scientist, a philosopher. I require regularity, order, peace. The world must not be allowed to disturb me, do you understand?'

'I've—I've come to make up the fire, sir,' stammered Will, not understanding anything.

The master gave him a swift black glance and began rocking backwards and forwards on his narrow feet. When he spoke, it was with the suddenness of a whip's cracking.

'Do you have a name?'

Will spoke as soon as he'd swallowed his heart back down out of his throat.

'Will, sir. Will Nunn.'

'Will,' repeated the master, musingly, as though tasting it. 'It is brief enough: simple enough: lacking in hissings and polysyllables.' Then he came even closer, so that Will could smell the ink and dust and ancient sweat that hung around him. The master peered into Will's face.

'Are you loyal?' he demanded, with a lick at his dry, pale lips.

'Why . . . why, yes, sir.'

The master turned abruptly away.

'Then make up the fire and get out.'

And so I learned my trade, my new trade, as a fighting man: *reveille, inspection, drill, exercises.*

Learned it well, too.

They gave me my own musket of oak and iron. You needed muscles just to lift it—but

26

lift it I did, hour after hour, day after day, loading, cleaning, marching, *reveille, inspection, drill, exercises* . . . until the heft of it grew sweet under my hands, and I did not disgrace my comrades.

The men's leaving jolted every part of life in the house out of its accustomed pattern. People who had slotted neatly together, every one in the right place at the right time, banged into each other, or found gaping holes where once there had been support. Everything was much harder for everyone, and Miss Winter, whiter and more fragile than ever, was always pattering anxiously into the kitchen to make sure that things would be done to time. It was, of course, her duty to see that the master was content, and Will did not really understand why these visits were the source of so much annoyance and offence: but Betty and Pamela and Mary packed their bags and left, all together; and Rosie declared that she might have gone with them, if she didn't have George to wait for.

'We're off to town,' said Betty, who had retrimmed her bonnet with a scarlet ribbon. 'There's a regiment there that'll pay well for service, I'll lay.'

'But how shall we manage?' asked Miss Winter, blinking timidly after their three determined figures as they marched away under the archway. 'How shall we keep the house running according to my brother's wishes? I must look into everything very closely. Perhaps there may be some work I can do myself. My brother does not require my company, after all.'

But this well-meaning resolution only caused more resentment.

'Why must the mistress interfere so all the time?' demanded Rosie, irritably. 'She's always prying and worriting. Why can she not get herself married and out of the way? I'm sure I'd be ashamed to be an old maid like her.'

Mrs Keen sighed.

'It's not easy to marry when you never see a man,' she said. 'Anyway, the mistress is not quite an old maid, yet. She is worn down with care, but she is much younger than the master. Why, she is only . . . yes, coming up for thirty.'

'Well,' said Rosie, grudgingly, 'I'm not surprised she's in a fidget all the time, with that hanging over her. I suppose I must pity her, then.'

Rosie took over the dairy and made lemon-bright pats of butter.

'We shall have some to take to market,' said Mrs Keen. 'That'll be as good as a holiday for us, Rosie.'

But suddenly the roads were no longer safe for travel. The rebels had had a victory, and it was said that the main road was blocked. Recently, the district had quite often seen armed men riding between the dusty roses that rambled through the hedges, though there was never a sign of George. Certainly letters had ceased to arrive, and the master's rents with them.

Miss Winter worried over her accounts.

'We will have to make savings,' she said. 'And we must be careful not to allow any waste, Mrs Keen.'

'Indeed, ma'am,' said Mrs Keen, folding her great pink arms. 'But there is no waste in my kitchen, I assure you. Why, Toby takes all he can for his dunghill, and Will eats the rest.'

Miss Winter looked rather nervously at Will, who blushed red as a beetroot with shame.

'He has grown very large,' she observed.

'Aye, he has, ma'am, and there's no filling him, either. Why, that jacket will not last him the year, the way he's shooting up.'

Will was too big altogether. Rosie tripped over his feet that very evening, and nearly upset a whole tray of puddings.

'You great homack!' she cried, as he leapt up and tried to push himself back out of the way into the plaster of the wall. 'Can't you watch where you put your great flat feet?'

But Will was watching something other than his feet: and he was frozen with the amazement and wonder of it. He discovered for the first time that he was taller than Rosie—inches taller, he was, when he stood up tall, as he was doing now.

And he also discovered, like rising buns of heavenly dough, the transfixing miracle of Rosie's breasts.

Chapter 6

The harvest was a fine one, though they were impossibly short-handed; and when the hunters' moon waxed once more the weather was bright and sharp after weeks of wild warm weather that had swelled the hard earth to squelching soddenness.

At long last there were orders from high up (higher, in fact, than we had ever seen). A battle, we heard. We nodded, business-like, for this was our purpose.

We marched, singing, each step together, to a field scattered with coats of another colour. Then we wheeled, made files, aimed, fired, just as we had a hundred times before. (Those muskets kicked like mules, but there, we were men enough to take it.) We stood shoulder to shoulder and fired, together, with the same hand, the same breath, the same aim.

The enemy, not so smart, was felled into a jumble.

Then orders came for us to march on.

The enemy fled ahead of us, so there was no need for us to fire again.

'Will! Give me a hand with this ladder!'

Will carefully laid down his chisel and went out into the courtyard. He had grown half a foot more in the last few months, and a good bit outwards, too, so that his large hands reached too far and knocked things over, and his heavy feet tripped him up.

But he was strong. He helped Mr Gilfry manhandle the heavy ladder up against the wall of the barn. The hunters' moon would shine today. Yes, thirteen moons, it was, exactly, since George had left.

Mr Gilfry got the ladder firmly grounded amongst the cobbles, and Will flicked a quick glance back over his shoulder. He'd been imagining hoofbeats since breakfast, but that sound must have been the wooden rails of the ladder knocking on the stones.

'Good lad,' said Mr Gilfry, his face ruddy and his barrel-chest heaving. 'Now, I'll go up, Will, and you step the ladder.'

Mr Gilfry retied the strings of his apron across his belly and lifted a muscular thigh. Will waited until Mr Gilfry's nailed boots had trodden purposefully past his eyes and then he stepped up on the bottom rung. During the summer ivy had begun to grow through the weatherboarding of the barn. It seemed impossible that the pale grey shoots could pull apart the wood, but they had done it, and set little fish-shapes of light swimming round in the darkness inside.

Thirteen moons, it was, exactly. So George might arrive at any moment. Will had imagined it lots of times. George would be Captain George—no, Captain *Gilfry*—and he'd bring such a file of fine men with him that Mrs Keen would be sent into a panic about feeding them all.

The ladder bounced a little under Will's feet. Mr Gilfry was tugging at the strong trailers of ivy. Will turned himself round and hitched his backside on a rung. Rosie had come out to hang some dish-cloths in a strip of the golden autumn sunshine. Will watched her bend down to the peg basket and then reach up to the line. Sometimes her skirts clung round her interestingly as she straightened up.

The ladder rocked a little and a bunch of leaves garnished with pale buds fell past Will's face and bounced slackly on the cobbles.

And then, out on the drive, Will really did hear something. It could well have been hooves, but what with all the scraping and screeching of timber above his head he couldn't be certain.

Rosie looked up, a peg between her lips.

A horse: yes, it was a horse. Will was almost sure of it.

He took one foot off the ladder and swung round to call up to Mr Gilfry.

'Mr Gilfry!' he called. 'I think—'

But Mr Gilfry was stretching to reach one last tendril of the marauding ivy—just a little further—and suddenly the ladder was moving. It was rearing up under Will's foot. The ladder paused stomach-chillingly on one rail for a long, long second . . . and then everything was staggering into disaster. Will, still hanging on to the ladder, was somehow falling sideways—and something colossally huge was falling down with him. At him.

Will flung himself out of its way. He hit the cold cobbles very hard and was curling round a bashed knee when the huge weight hit the ground beside him. It landed with a thud and a grunt of heavy breath.

'Mr Gilfry!' someone shouted. 'Will!'

But now there was something else toppling down at him: Will, panic-stricken, kicked out half-blindly at it. It banged against his ankle, knocked him resoundingly on the forehead, and clattered to a rest. Will gave out a cry and rolled away.

Footsteps were running towards him across the cobbles—and then there was a swishing draught of skirts and they went past. Will miserably shook away the ringing in his head, pushed himself up on his elbow, and blinked round.

Rosie was kneeling on the cobbles. She was stroking Mr Gilfry's broad back cautiously, and from a distance, as one might a skittery horse.

'Are you all right?' she was saying. 'Oh, please, Mr Gilfry, can you speak to me?'

Will blinked twice more and got unsteadily and by stages to his feet. He hardly dared breathe in case he fell to pieces. He staggered forward a step or two so he could see the figure on the ground.

Mr Gilfry's hair, always so neat, so smart, had fallen down over his forehead. There was a trickle of crimson blood running along his cheek.

Will couldn't believe it. Mr Gilfry was the most solid thing in the world. Mr Gilfry was indestructible.

But Mr Gilfry's leg was wrong. Will shuddered and winced away at the sight of it. It was lying along the ground, as massive as a ham—but the foot was pointing in the wrong direction and Will knew in his guts that it was broken.

'We must get help,' said Rosie, breathlessly, still stroking Mr Gilfry's hard brown back. 'Mrs Keen will know what to do. Go and get Mrs Keen, Will.'

Let it be all right, Will thought, as he lurched dizzily across the yard. *Let it be all right. Let Mr Gilfry get up and not be hurt. Let him put all the blame on me, just so long as he's all right.*

The kitchen door opened before he reached it, and Mrs Keen's wide white bosom pushed itself out of the shadows.

'What's all this noise, Will?' she asked. 'You don't want to be disturbing the master, or—'

And then she saw the shape on the cobbles. She gasped—and then she was gathering up handfuls of skirts and running, properly running, with her pink woollen stockings showing above her shabby slippers and her cap-strings strung out along the way she'd come.

She lowered herself ponderously onto the cobbles and took Mr Gilfry's hand. She began talking urgently, softly, relentlessly, just as Rosie had done.

Will stood and was afraid. With that rock of a body motionless, with the two women round it, tending to it, he felt suddenly much too small: small, because he was afraid and ignorant and useless.

And then there was a movement. In the shadows of the archway shone a gleam of bronze—a horse's great head. Will's heart jumped, and a great hope spouted inside him like a spring.

Thirteen moons. Yes. It was just thirteen moons. And now out of the shadows came the muscular shoulders of the horse, gleaming in the warm sunshine. And yes, there was someone leading it. Will's heart jumped with gratitude. He ran across the yard and the horse tossed up its head so that the young man's head was jerked up, too, to show a flash of paler skin.

But it was not George.

More noise. More noise. I will not have it.

I must take steps to protect myself, to protect the order of things.

They must all be brought to heel.

Chapter 7

Now, by the strange magnetism of disaster, other people were arriving. First there was young Sam, all eyes and mouth; and here was Miss Winter, her face thin with alarm.

Toby hastily led the great liver chestnut horse into the courtyard. His pink face was glowing with hurry and anxiety.

Toby. It was just Toby. Of course it was.

Just for a moment Will had a vision of them all, as if he was up in the master's tower. There was the courtyard, and there, spread upon it like little flowers, or like the plates and dishes on the dinner-table, were the people, all arranged.

But he was in the wrong place, somehow, spoiling the pattern.

Toby's eyes passed unheedingly over Mr Gilfry and on to Miss Winter.

'Here, ma'am,' he said. 'There's a rare amount of trouble in the village. They say there've been troops riding through, and that the King's men are beaten back. They reckon there's a big battle brewing and the rebels will be here in a couple of days.'

A rustle passed through them, as when hens

first glimpse a fox. Mrs Keen heaved herself hastily round to stare at Toby.

'Rebels?' echoed Miss Winter, shocked into immobility.

Toby's blue eyes were bright with urgency and importance.

'Yes, ma'am. There's been a battle up north, and they'll be here before long, they're saying. Half the village is packed up already into carts and barrows and all sorts, and the rest is scrabbling round like blind puppies.'

Miss Winter put up her hands to her thin throat.

'Rebels? Here?' she said. 'But they cannot come through here. The master—'

'But there's no one to stop them, ma'am,' said Toby, urgently. 'The King's men are all beaten back. Those rebels will be here before we know it, raping and pillaging. We must get away, all of us, and be off. We must load up the wagon.'

Mr Gilfry had propped himself up on one elbow and was dabbing blood off his face with his handkerchief. His face was the colour of planed deal.

Mrs Keen, kneeling beside him, spoke up.

'And here's Mr Gilfry's fallen off the ladder, if you please, ma'am, and I'm afraid he's badly hurt.'

Miss Winter seemed to notice for the first time that he was on the ground.

'What? Gilfry? But we cannot manage without him. No one else can chop the firewood as my brother likes it. Surely he can sit up?'

Mr Gilfry thought about it. Then he pushed against the cobbles with his great hands, winced, and tried again, twisting round to face his useless leg. It was a sort of comfort to see him more upright.

Mrs Keen put a restraining hand on Mr Gilfry's arm.

'His leg will need to be set, Miss Winter,' she said, apologetically. 'For it's broke, for certain.'

Toby was walking round in circles shaking his heavy chin.

'You won't find the apothecary at home,' he said. 'I've just seen his cart setting off piled high, and his Jem a-closing of his gate.'

Miss Winter turned from one to the other of them.

'But then what can we do? What can we do?'

'We've got to go,' said Toby, earnestly. 'I tell you, there's rebels coming. They'll be burning and looting and raping. They say they cut off the right hand of any man they see.'

Miss Winter took a great gasping breath.

'Then I shall have to tell the master,' she said, going quite white. 'At least . . . but I cannot keep this from him. I cannot. He must give orders as to what's to be done.'

And she hastened back into the house.

'And I'm off to pack,' said Toby. 'They say the rebels can't be here for a day or two yet, for they've their guns to move, but there's no point in taking chances.'

He hurried away as fast as his legs would take

him, and the others were left grouped round the big figure on the ground. Mrs Keen gave a long shuddering sigh.

'Oh, how can we bear this?' she said. ''Tis bad enough that our men are away, without news like this, of killing and battles. Oh, Mr Gilfry, what are we to do?'

But then she shook herself and began to roll up her pink sleeves over her beefy arms.

'We must manage, that's all,' she went on. 'We must carry on and hope. And being a cook I've plenty of experience with bones and joints, after all. Rosie, you fetch some blankets, if you please.'

'We could carry Mr Gilfry in on the wheelbarrow!' piped up young Sam, very excited, trying to be as solemn as the grown-ups, and failing by a mile.

Rosie, running off in search of blankets, gave her brother a perfunctory cuff for speaking out of his place.

Mrs Keen looked round, and fixed on Will.

'Now,' she said resolutely. 'I shall need the help of your strong arms, Will.'

They carried Mr Gilfry into the scullery on a hurdle, and Mrs Keen set his leg. Rosie stationed herself bravely at Mrs Keen's elbow and handed things. Will, miserable and in terror, did as he was bid and tried not even to think about being sick, even when Mr Gilfry was himself.

When Will returned from rinsing out the bowl he found Mr Gilfry alone, except for Rosie, who was hurriedly folding soft sheep-coloured blankets.

'Will,' said Mr Gilfry, 'there is an old bath chair in the back of the barn. You must get it out and fix it up so I can use it.'

'Begging your pardon,' said Rosie, 'but should you not rest, Mr Gilfry?'

He rolled a powerful blue eye at her.

'If there are rebels coming there is no time for any of us to rest,' he said.

Chapter 8

The bath chair had been designed for some spindly and decaying member of the Family, and Mr Gilfry, wedged in it with a plank underneath him to support his leg, looked like a blacksmith on a chamber pot. It served, however, to get him back out into the yard. Mr Gilfry was a respectable man, a good man, but he had a sharp edge to him, and, just now, the sharp edge was pointing outwards.

'So where's Toby?' he demanded, testily.

Will looked around rather helplessly.

'I can't rightly say, Mr Gilfry. Packing, I think.'

'Packing? Packing? And how can we pack when we can't roll out the wagon without him?'

'Gilfry! Gilfry!'

And here was Miss Winter trotting over the cobbles towards them, as nervous as a hen.

'I'll need some packing cases,' she said. 'And my spinet will have to be taken to pieces.'

Mr Gilfry made several attempts at getting up before he remembered he wasn't capable of doing it.

'You must remember we've only two horses to put to the wagon, ma'am,' he pointed out. 'We won't be able to take much.'

41

Miss Winter looked baffled, and even more alarmed.

'But we must take my spinet. My brother likes to hear it when there is no moon. Oh, and I must tell Mrs Keen to be sure to pack the master's cup and plate separately from everything else, so they are not contaminated.'

Mr Gilfry sighed, and leant back in his chair:

'All that will take time, ma'am. And we can't afford it.'

'I know, I know. We must get everything done as quickly as we can. We will leave here at dawn tomorrow, so we can be at the Red House by dusk.'

Mr Gilfry grunted.

'That'll be a fair step, ma'am.'

'Yes, indeed, but it is a place my brother knows, which is a great advantage. It is sited well away from the main road, too, so it should be safe. And my brother has been paying a steward to keep it in good order.'

There were heavy footsteps and Toby appeared round the corner from the kitchen garden. He had a pack on his back and a spade in his hand.

'Are we ready to go, then?' he asked.

The woman speaks too fast. The words rattle round her empty skull, clattering, clattering. The war. Rebels. She does not understand how small they are.

She wishes for change.

But that would disturb me. So I shall not allow it.

The house was like a stirred-up ants' nest, with piled-high people scurrying backwards and forwards from the cold courtyard.

Will was just in time to open the door to the laundry for Rosie. She went in and threw her nose-grazing heap of blankets onto the floor.

'Oh, but I've been running up and down those stairs until my legs ache,' she said. 'There's so much it'd be foolish to leave behind, but when I think of those rebels I just want to fling it all away and make a run for it.'

'Can I help you?' asked Will, humbly.

Rosie snorted.

'I rather doubt it, Will,' she said, and bustled off again, scattering the coppery hens as she went.

Will sighed, and went back to lugging a packing case up the stairs. Of course Rosie didn't want him bothering around her, he told himself, as he heaved the unwieldy thing from step to step. Why, Rosie was George's sweetheart. George, who was Mr Gilfry's son, and a bright brave soldier. George, who'd be able to provide for Rosie all her life long. That was what Rosie wanted, someone clever who could keep her in comfort, and Will had no call to think about her, nor ever would have.

'*You! Will Nunn!*'

Will jumped so violently that the case nearly lurched out of his clutching fingers and back down the stairs. A sharp nose was jutting fiercely out of the awful darkness behind the tower-door tapestry.

'Up here, boy! Up here! Come!'

Will suddenly discovered that shifting packing cases was actually not such a bad job. He bumped the thing up the last step, and then climbed reluctantly after the master up the bone-white stairs.

'Here, here!'

The master's head was shooting excitedly backwards and forwards on his thin neck. 'There is a fault with my telescope. I was adjusting the elevation, ready for tonight's observation, and this came away.'

The master was holding something out to him, a little bright wheel.

Will, all the time aware of the ticking clock that marked the advance of the rebel forces, took the wheel in his hand. It was made of turned brass, and there was a screw thread on the shaft. There was no sign of any damage to it.

'There is a hole, here, where it fitted.'

There was only one thing Will could think of to do, so he did it. He put the shaft delicately into the hole and twisted the wheel.

It went in sweetly and easily.

'Ha! But is it working? Is it? Is it?'

Will hadn't a clue.

'Well, look through the eyepiece!' urged the master, impatiently, flapping a thin hand at the end of the tube. 'Check it, check it!'

Will bowed his head to the end of the tube, caught a flash of light, and went closer still, until his eyelashes tickled.

A blur of grey and darkness, like a muddy raindrop.

'Well? What can you see? What can you see?'

'Just mist, sir.'

'So turn the wheel, boy! Turn it, turn it!'

Will felt for it and turned it. The mist squirmed, expanded and got mistier still. So he turned it the other way and the mists converged until . . .

He gasped. He could see Rosie hurrying up the path, but somehow she seemed only an arm's length away. He could see the little clouds of breath round her pink lips. He could see her white shawl, pulled snugly round her shoulders. He could watch her, close, close, without her knowing anything of it. Will looked away from the image in amazement, took a deep breath, and then ducked back to look again.

It was a new picture, this time, but that might have been because he'd knocked the tube a little. Now he could see Toby's round brown backside. Toby was throwing a covering over one of the compost heaps. There was an angry mound of a pink pimple on the back of his neck.

'Well? Well, boy? Is it functioning?'

Will stood up, a little dazed.

'I think so, sir.'

The master shuffled forward and lowered his eye to the end of the tube. Then he grunted and twiddled at the focusing wheel.

'Your eyes are different from mine. They are not so worn with close work. Ah!'

It was not Will's place to ask questions, but he heard himself blurt out:

'Is it real, what it shows us, sir?'

The master looked across lopsidedly from the tube.

'Certainly. This is a telescope: the first part of the word, *tele*, signifies distance, and the second, *scope*, vision. Do you understand?'

Will could not in conscience commit himself to anything so definite.

'So Rosie—and the kitchen garden—they were truly as I saw them?'

The master began mumbling, and twitching the telescope to and fro.

'My interest is in the celestial bodies—in the patterns of the night sky, but—yes. Yes, there is a youth doing something agricultural. Quite real.'

He stood up as far as his stoop would allow, and his twitchiness was suddenly shot with rage.

'I will not have it!' he snapped. 'This room has been my refuge. And now this war arrives, which knows nothing of my work and cares less, and it would turn me out. Out of my own house!'

Will took an apprehensive step back from the vicious spittle that shot from the master's pale lips.

'What respect does the world have for a mind such as mine?' the master went on. 'Can it come close to comprehending its value? No, no, they hop along with their endless trivial garbage—drudgery and defeat and disease—forcing itself upon me. Disturbing my mind. Yes, shooting it full of ragged holes. My mind,' he went on, thoughtfully now, 'my fine mind, is full of holes . . . Boy!'

'Yes, sir?' gulped Will.

'Destroy it. Destroy the apparatus. The telescope. Destroy it.'

Will flinched before the red glint in the master's black eyes.

'Don't you see?' the master demanded. 'Don't you see how it contaminates me? How it brings confusion, the war, close? Yes, yes, it shows the patterns of the sky, but it is not selective. It lures me in, taints me, betrays me. Take it apart! I order you! Take it apart!'

Loosening the wing-nuts collapsed the tripod to a bundle of sticks. Will glanced up, but the master was walking up and down muttering to himself, unnoticing.

The telescope was a beautiful thing. It was joined together with gleaming screw-threads, and there were close-fitting tubes that glided on the merest film of oil; and within them were endlessly buffed lenses. Will wondered at the skill of it. He laid each piece reverently on the rich green leather-covered table, and he felt as if he were laying out something dead.

'Is it done?' demanded a voice like a whiplash behind him.

'Yes, sir,' said Will, sadly.

'That will stop it, then. That will stop the war coming. Yes. Good. Now I am safe. The whole house is safe.'

The master sat himself down at his desk, drew out a magnifying glass from a drawer, and began to study one of the lenses of the telescope.

'Regularity,' he muttered. 'Pattern and form. Perfection, in a way.'

Will, terrified and uncomprehending, backed silently out.

We marched into the open arms of a city.

I'd never seen anything like it: houses, people, whole streets, cheering. We marched chest by chest, step by step, victors, as proud and bright as peacocks.

The people put out their best to honour us. Oh, that was a night, that was (though, to be sure, I don't remember it as plainly as I might). At home, when I was a boy, Mr Keen poured out beer so weak I'd hardly taste it. But now I was a man.

The girls were all round us. There was a pretty one who smiled at me. So I obliged her. Aye, I was a man, sure enough.

Oh, the sweets of victory . . .

. . . and then, the next groaning, head-splitting day, the jolting, thumping march with my whey-faced comrades towards the next one.

Chapter 9

The great blue and yellow wagon had been put under shelter for the winter.

'It's a wreck,' said Toby, shaking his head. 'It'll fall to pieces the minute we try to shift it, that will.'

Will tried to be hopeful. It was true that the wagon should have had several of the strakes on the off back wheel replaced, but generally it looked solid. Will picked up the heavy chocks that held the wagon in its place and threw them up inside the wagon.

'Ready?' he said. 'Push!'

It took all their strength to heave the wagon over the hump of the first cobble, but then it gathered momentum and all they had to do was keep the thing going.

'Whoa!' said Mr Gilfry, from his bath chair. 'That'll do, now, lads.'

Will and Toby stood and puffed a mist of white breath into the courtyard.

'All right,' said Mr Gilfry. 'No time for lazing about. You must bring down the cases.'

Even with Toby to help, it was all but impossible to manoeuvre the heavy cases down the stairs.

'What has the mistress put in this thing?' gasped Toby, his face red with straining and his boils redder still.

Will pushed back his hair and discovered a cobweb. He must have picked that up when he was searching the darkest shelves at the back of the barn for nails to close the packing cases. He'd found a whole jar of them. They were rusty and crooked, but straightening them had been an easy job that Mr Gilfry could do from his chair.

It suddenly struck Will as strange that the easy jobs were now for Mr Gilfry.

Miss Winter was down in the courtyard, scurrying anxiously backwards and forwards.

'Which case is that?' she asked, pattering forward in a flutter of worry. 'I marked them with chalk.'

Will looked at his hands. Chalk? He was covered in it—and all down his jacket, too. He dabbed shamefacedly at the white dust and only succeeded in cleaning his hands.

Miss Winter looked ready to cry at the sight of it.

'But what will my brother do if I cannot find things when he needs them? Let me see. Oh, thank providence, I can just make out the letters.'

She delved swiftly into her blue pocket, pinched out a stick of chalk, and made some new swirling squiggles on the case.

'There,' she said. 'That's clear again. Second Best China. And now the window must be taken out.'

Will blinked.

'The *window*, ma'am?'

'Yes, the stained-glass window. It is a favourite of my brother's. We cannot possibly leave it.'

And she pattered away in a trail of business.

There was a pause while Will and Toby looked at each other.

'*Second Best China*,' Toby echoed, sadly. 'Not now, it's not, I'll warrant. It'll be *fifth* best china, the way we've been crashing that case about. The world's first thousand-piece tea set!'

Will, wincing, remembered the way they'd banged it on the ceiling at the turn of the stairs, and the way they'd managed to whack it against the door-frame when they were trying to manoeuvre the thing out into the courtyard.

'Ah well,' said Toby. 'She'll most probably think it was all rattled to pieces on the journey. What else is to go on the wagon?'

'I don't know,' Will admitted. 'Not much more, because we're nearly full up. I would have thought we'd have been packing pans and buckets, but the mistress is most agitated about the master's things.'

Toby sighed deeply.

'They're all mad,' he announced. 'Quality, they're all the same. The master's plain insane, and the poor mistress is too scared silly of him to realize. That's what happens when people have no contact with the earth. Here we are with murdering rebels coming to slice us open, and what's their first thought? Tea sets! They don't understand how the world works.'

Will, expecting a thunderbolt, ducked away from the sky. How could Toby say such things of the family, who clothed them and kept them from starving? Of the master, who had knowledge far, far beyond comprehension?

'They do not see common things in use, you see,' went on Toby, shaking his head. 'They see food on their plates, but they don't consider where it has come from.' He regarded the steep slope up the ramp to the wagon and spat on his hands. 'Well, they'll all be realizing it soon,' he said, with mournful satisfaction. 'If we live that long. Yes, they'll be aware of the advantages of a carefully tended dunghill once they're deprived of the benefits of it, you mark my words.'

Taking down the window took two precious hours of Will's and Toby's time. It was made in panels that fitted between the graceful branches of the stonework: but the panels, though small, were still heavy, what with all the lead that held them together.

Will scraped away the cement that held the panels in place, and untwisted the copper wire that tied them to the iron bars that fitted across the stonework. The soldier lost first his silver legs, and then his body, until only his head hung shining against the emerald hills.

Toby stacked the panels on the landing floor. The air buffeted in at them cruelly now there was a gaping hole where the window should have been, numbing their fingers and turning their sweat to ice.

'Did you hear that?' Toby asked, suddenly.

Will peered past the window to the lemon and copper and crimson of the trees.

'I heard something,' he said. 'Mrs Keen's beating a rug, maybe. She always beats rugs when she's upset, and she's powerful upset about having to leave her jelly moulds.'

There was another bang, a flat, dry bang, like a flour sack dropping onto the cobbles. Then there was another, and another, and another: not regularly spaced, but stumbling, almost casual.

'Those are cannons, they are,' said Toby, in sudden realization. 'Look, let's be off, Will. Just the two of us. We'll travel faster if we don't go with the others. And I won't be so scared if I have company.'

An icy gust skirled through the stone fluting and set a painting on the wall beside Will rocking on its purple cord.

Rosie poked her head round the corner.

'Can't someone close that door?' she asked. 'Because there's a terrible—oh!'

Will tried as hard as he could not to stare at the tiny gathers that clung so roundly to Rosie's bosoms.

'You're taking the window out,' she said, in flat surprise.

Will nodded, for his tongue had become stuck to the top of his mouth.

'*Just* what we'll be needing with us, half a ton of coloured glass,' said Rosie, too weary even to be properly annoyed.

There were half a dozen more thumps. Underneath them, Mrs Keen was hastening across the yard towards the archway.

Rosie turned to Will, almost accusingly.

'Those are guns, aren't they?'

Will swallowed hard, partly with fear, but with excitement, too.

'I think they are,' he said.

Chapter 10

Mr Gilfry shifted himself cautiously in his chair. From the way Rosie and Mrs Keen kept fussing around him, Will guessed that he must be in a lot of pain. Will wondered how the women knew.

'There's no real choice but to go along the main road,' Mr Gilfry told Will, a stubby finger on the map. 'Though it's hardly a sensible thing to load all our valuables onto a wagon and then drive it between a couple of armies.'

There was a tacking of heels from the courtyard and the doorway was darkened by a thin figure.

'Gilfry? Are you there?'

Mr Gilfry leaned forward, scrabbled his hands a little, and then sat back again with a sigh.

'You will have to build an enclosed seat on the wagon for the master,' said Miss Winter.

Will, trying his best to merge with the wall, gave Mr Gilfry a glance. A seat?

Mr Gilfry sat, hugely immovable and hugely patient, while somehow making it quite clear that patience was necessary.

'Will,' he said, 'show Miss Winter the wagon, if you please.'

It didn't please Will in the slightest—he'd much rather have hidden himself in the woodpile until she'd gone—but he shifted himself along.

The wagon was full. More than full, indeed, for it was packed so high in the centre that Will had had to tie ropes across to stop things sliding off.

Miss Winter stared at it blankly.

'But the master would never . . . ' she began. And, really, he would not. Will might have ridden on top of that great pile of boxes and bales, but you could not possibly expect a lady or gentleman to do the same. Will had a vision of Miss Winter squirming and kicking her way up the top of the load: and then, fascinated and revolted, he steered his mind away again.

'But what can we do?' Miss Winter was asking.

Will kept quiet.

Miss Winter slipped round the wagon, scattering the russet hens as she went.

'And what can we do about the silver? I suppose we must carry it ourselves. Both Rosie and Mrs Keen are sturdy enough, and they are used to heavy work. They will not notice the extra weight, perhaps.'

Rosie had tried out the weight of her own pack earlier: the straps had dug hard into her soft shoulders.

'I could carry some of that,' Will had offered, hesitantly. 'I haven't got anything of my own to carry, Rosie, save a few bits of clothes, and my tools.'

'Don't be foolish,' Rosie had said, but only wearily.

'I'd—I'd be careful with your things,' Will had mumbled; and Rosie had looked at him—and then she'd actually smiled.

'You great fool,' she'd said, though not unkindly. 'We can't have you staggering about under the weight of a heavy pack. We need you free to help Sam. He's still young, and he'll have the horses to see to.'

It was certain that Sam would need help. Will came across him, later, wrestling fiercely to free a pitchfork of hay that he'd managed to get caught up in some guttering. Sam was hardly strong enough to lift the fork itself, let alone the hay on the end of it.

'You should ask Toby to let you use his barrow,' suggested Will, rescuing him, though he had not a minute to spare. Sam was a clever lad, but he was only ten years old and still really too small for heavy work.

'But that's full of muck, most of the time, Will,' Sam had objected. 'I wouldn't ask a horse to eat anything that'd even been near it.'

'I must think,' said Miss Winter, clenching her thin fists. 'What can be done? What *can* be done? My brother will never walk; but he *must* walk. He does not realize the danger, for I have always protected him from what has been happening in the outside world. But I cannot protect him any longer. *I cannot.*'

Will glanced at the great clock. Half past four. Twelve stained-glass panels stacked up on the landing, and no place for them on the wagon, any more than there was place for the master. And all the time the rebels were getting closer with their guns and swords and fierce strength. Closer to the house; closer to Rosie.

Will would hide the panels somewhere and hope no one thought any more about them.

He left Miss Winter dithering and ran up hastily between the black pinnacles of the staircase with hardly a thought for its beauty.

When I was young, before I was a man, sometimes there was dancing. Mr Keen would make his fiddle sing (ironwood for the bow, and maple, ebony, and deal for the fiddle—not that it matters) and men and maids would line up and step out smartly.

I danced with Rosie. She was the smartest of the lot, was Rosie.

That battle was like that, to begin with. Two lines, ready: bugles and drums, music to make your heart leap. We stepped, we stopped, we kept time to the beat.

We were well drilled—we were drilled through the ears, to be honest, with constant bellowing, until there was a hole in our heads to slot our orders in.

Advance! was the word. So of course we did. Some fell, but that was neither here nor there.

And then we met, and I lost sight of most things. It was a rare thing, that fighting . . .

being free. Oh, yes. Spending yourself without a thought beyond that minute. The greatest freedom you could imagine. I fought with all my strength, I did, right until it was over and we were all heroes again.

Chapter 11

'Will Nunn!'

Will, bent over the glass panels on the landing, jumped guiltily.

'Yes, sir?'

The mauves and greens of the tapestry twitched, and behind it two pinpoints of light gleamed amidst the darkness of the tower stairs.

'I need—'

But then the beetle-shape of the master lurched hastily forward into the light.

'Who did this?' he demanded, his voice shrill with anger. 'Who took out the glass? Who did it?'

'It—it's to save it from the rebels, sir,' said Will, with a gulp.

The little man stamped his foot, a swift percussion of rage.

'Put it back up!' he snapped, spitting like a whip. 'Put it back up!'

Will tried for a long moment to imagine how that might be possible, but it would soon be getting dark, and they were leaving at first light.

The master was shifting from leg to leg, breathing hard and muttering.

'My sister, this household. They are conspiring to drive me out of my mind. But they shall not succeed. Oh no, I am determined that they shall not.'

He bent almost hungrily over the stack of panels, edging his fingers under the glass.

Then he let out a small sound that might almost have been a chuckle.

'Look! Look! My fingers are stained. Red and yellow. Red and cobalt. Extraordinary. Extraordinary.'

He turned to the gaping hole that was the window. Through it could be seen a web of black branches and flaming leaves, and even, far away, a glimpse of the main road. 'Yes, yes, of course,' he said. 'I have never known what was through the window, what was hidden by it. Yes. Boy!'

'Yes, sir?'

'These panels—bring them up to the tower.'

Will's back groaned at the thought of lifting them. Every time, with a final back-clenching effort, he'd heaved something up the ramp onto the wagon, he'd found himself actually feeling sorry for the vehicle itself, in the same way he would feel sorry for an over-laden donkey.

Surely the wagon would not stand up to the repeated jolts of the cobbles in the courtyard, let alone the precipitous lurchings along the wheel-ruts of the road.

'Hurry up, hurry up!'

The master's thin nose poked pinkly at him out of the blackness behind the tapestry curtain.

'William!'

And here was Miss Winter calling him, too. Her heels were tripping hastily along the corridor.

'Here is something else that must go on the wagon, William.'

She was clutching a mahogany frame. Will's heart sank. *Nothing* else could go on the wagon. Nothing at all.

The master shot back out of the staircase, and it was as if he had brought a patch of darkness with him.

'What now? What now?' he demanded.

Miss Winter flinched, but swept into a rapid explanation.

'It is this mirror,' she said. 'Our mother's mirror. I know you would not like to be without it.'

She turned it round to show the master the two narrow mirrors that folded over and met in the middle of the biggest one.

He came forward and took it from her.

'I remember, I remember,' he muttered.

The side mirrors fell open a little in his hands, so the mirrors formed most of a triangle. He looked down at them, and his face sharpened.

'Like a tunnel,' he said, frowning. 'Yes, yes, a tunnel of reflections going on to infinity. Back and forth, back and forth, dashing from one surface to the other. Look here, sister. A tunnel. But going—where?'

Miss Winter wrinkled her brow.

'But it does not go anywhere,' she said; and he let out a bark of laughter.

'How lacking in order is the female brain! How could a tunnel go nowhere? Plainly impossible. And yet . . . '

'I know this mirror is important,' said Miss Winter. 'I remember how, when I was very young, you would put a picture of a soldier between the mirrors to give the illusion of a whole army, or perhaps a picture of a star to make a little universe.'

The master grunted, scowling with thought.

'An illusion? Was that all it was, hey?'

Miss Winter blinked at him timidly.

'Well, brother, like all children we took great pleasure in imaginary things such as tales, and pictures in the fire.'

The master shook his head, and hugged the mirror to his chest.

'But the pleasure—that was not an illusion,' he said.

He was rocking backwards and forwards on his shabby black shoes, frowning at nothing. Will, forgotten and uncomprehending, wondered if he might be able to slip away. Mr Gilfry would be waiting for him, and he had so very many things still to do.

Through the window came the decaying smell of autumn: of coral mushrooms and bronzing leaves. And just coming into sight round the bend in the road were . . .

'Horses, ma'am!' Will blurted out. 'Soldiers, on the road!'

Miss Winter spun round.

'Arthur! Look! Look!'

He did look up, then, though without catching the edge of her excitement.

'Yes, yes. Those are soldiers, sister. But if you had not taken the window down, they would not be there.'

Miss Winter turned to him and actually laid a hand on his greasy sleeve.

'Listen to me,' she said, almost pleadingly. 'Listen. There are soldiers on the road. Don't you see? Soon there will be more, and they will be the enemy. They will come here, and if they find us they will kill us. We must leave this house.'

Will almost said something, even though it was not his place. Yes, the house had thick walls and sturdy doors, but the outside world was only a few feet away. It was closer than that, even: as close as the thickness of their eyelids.

The master jerked his wrist viciously out of her grasp and took a step backwards, bent and black, his head jutting aggressively forwards.

'Oh no, oh no,' he said. 'You shall not trick me, sister. Do not imagine you have the guile to deceive me. The world shall stay outside, where it belongs. I shall not have it in here. You know . . . you know it disturbs my mind, sister. It has always disturbed my mind.'

Miss Winter put out a beseeching hand—but then let it fall to her side.

'But I will look after you,' she said, almost coaxingly. 'You know I have always looked after you. Everything that is important to you is packed and ready. There would be nothing to fear.'

But the master rocked on his feet faster still, and twin spots of red appeared on the pallor of his cheeks.

'There would be many things,' he said. 'Coming. Coming. Always there are things around. Disturbances. Ugly things. One cannot see the pattern, one is pushed about, hurt, damaged. I would be damaged. No, I shall stay here and you shall stay with me. You and the boy. You shall stay and keep house for me and we shall be safe from everything.'

But Miss Winter put up her thin hands to her ears.

'No,' she said. 'I cannot. I have given you everything else. I have given you everything I have, but this time you must give way. This is too much for ourselves alone, do you understand? There is an army coming. Rebels. You keep yourself apart from it all, but there is news continually of the dreadful things that happen when they come. Would you have us all killed? We have stayed and packed up everything we can to make you comfortable, but we must leave first thing tomorrow. And . . . and we shall only be going to the Red House. You know the Red House, brother. It is quiet, there, away from the road and all the comings and goings. Why, we were there as children, sometimes.'

The road through the window was empty, now, and the rumbling of the horses' hooves was only a growling in the distance. Miss Winter stood and faced her brother, and their faces became almost mirror-images of each other; thin-nosed, filled with long-nursed needs and anxieties.

'I always knew you sought to destroy me,' said the master, with spitting bitterness. 'But I shall have the whip-hand of you.'

And Miss Winter turned with a whisk of blue skirts and ran away down the corridor.

The master watched her go. He had a strange new light in his eye.

'Go and get your tools,' he ordered Will. 'And then bring a panel of the coloured glass up to the tower.'

'Yes, sir,' said Will. Then, hesitantly, he added: 'Shall I take the mistress's mirror for you, sir?'

The master just paused for a moment, the light illuminating his bony fingers as they clasped the frame of the mirror.

'No. It is mine,' he said harshly. 'The mistress is too ignorant to understand how to use it.'

And then he turned again and merged lurchingly into the darkness.

Chapter 12

Will laid the stained-glass panel on the green leather of the master's desk beside the tubes and lenses which had once been the telescope. The leather took all the colour from the glass and left it ugly.

'Have you your tools, boy?'

Will approached warily. He could almost feel the secrets in the walls leaning in on him, smothering him.

'What is it you wish me to do, sir?'

'This coloured glass. Smash it.'

Will gasped.

'But—sir—'

'Have you a hammer? Hey?'

Will wished there was someone who might come and help him; but he was alone. He pulled open the cord at the top of his tool bag.

They were old tools, second- or third-hand, but they were well-wrapped, and greased and sharp. The hammer was at the bottom, well away from the delicate steel-tipped blades of his three chisels. Will picked it out and felt its friendly settle in his hand.

'That's it, boy. That's it. Give it to me.'

Will hesitated. Mr Gilfry had given him a

sonorous lecture with every precious item that had been added to his tool kit. *Never lend your tools*, he'd said. They were to be his companions for life, and he must be able to trust them. Another man's holding of them might send them out of true, make them sit awkwardly in his fingers.

'What is it you want done, sir?' he asked.

The master's lean hand flapped on the desk. 'I need small pieces of glass. Little, jagged pieces, no more than a quarter of an inch long. But not dust, you understand. Little jewels, to hold the light.'

Will picked up a corner of the glass panel and the colours bloomed over his skin. There was a border of red and blue squares: bluer, redder, than anything, a vividness to make a kingfisher shy. And inside was the shouting green of the grassy mound on which the soldier stood. Will ran his fingers under the glass. Here was a buttercup, and a daisy, and a marigold that had popped up clean out of season. Every colour there could be, chiming as clear and clean as a ring of bells.

Will lifted the hammer—and paused.

'Will you really have me break it, sir?'

The master darted him a black glance.

'Yes, yes! Get on with it!'

Will raised the hammer, took aim—and paused again.

'If I break it, sir, it won't go back in the window,' he said, almost desperately. 'You'll not be able to shut out the world any more.'

But the master smiled, and his eyes sparkled darkly over his thin lips and narrow nose.

'It is the only way,' he said, musingly. 'The only hope . . . you would not understand.'

'No, sir,' said Will; and he was glad to recognize that it was beyond him. He raised the hammer and brought it down sharply on the glowing glass.

The lead was even softer than he'd expected. The strips warped and stretched so that some of the pieces of glass came loose. The master was stretching out a long white wrist and seizing them as they fell. A green piece, first, and then one of the richest ruby, and then a brazen yellow.

'Good,' he muttered, holding first one piece than another up to the bluing light from the window. 'Bright, clear. Good. But too big yet.' He put the pieces back down on the desk. 'Smash them. Smash them.'

That would damage the window beyond hope. It would scar the leather of the desk, too—but then this was the master's wish, and in any case Will was too stupid and ignorant to understand. He brought the hammer down sharply once more, making the little silver knife on the table jump; and again, and again.

'Good, good.'

The master was pawing over the bright splinters as if they were real jewels. Then he looked up, and his mouth was moist and his eyes lit with excitement. 'Now the mirror,' he said. 'The mirror must be broken, too.'

Three mirrors: bad luck for as long as Will could imagine. But then Will was only a bastard and a pauper, of no account to anybody. What did it matter what his luck was? He pulled at the paper tape which hid the tacks that held the mirror in place.

The master's thin breath left wisps of warmth on Will's fingers.

'One should give us area enough,' said the master.

Seven years' bad luck, then: until Will was of age. But that was only if he lived that long.

The master had found one of the tubes from the dismantled telescope and was rolling it between his bony fingers.

'We will need three pieces of mirror,' he muttered. 'They will each need to be rectangular and elongated. And of precise size. How is that to be done?'

Will had seen Mr Gilfry cutting glass, once, after George had broken a pane with a catapult.

That seemed a long time ago: when they were both children.

'With a diamond, sir,' said Will, diffidently.

The master threw a black glance almost at Will, and nodded, and drew a ring off a withering finger.

'Here,' he said.

There was an edge Will could use to mark the glass. He measured the mirror twice, and then scored it so the diamond just bit, as Mr Gilfry had showed him. The glass showed a faint dull mark like a skater left in the ice. Will picked the mirror up, pushed steadily down with his thumbs and upwards with his fingers, and the glass split exactly along the line he'd marked. He took a deep breath of surprise and accomplishment and bent back down to his task.

'The edges will be sharp, sir,' said Will, standing up at long last and pushing back his hair.

'Yes, yes, of course. Pass me that lens, boy. There. That's right. That's right. And that other one, by the inkwell. Now.'

Will watched the master's thin fingers. They were clumsy, unpractised, but the mind behind them knew what it was about. A lens was slotted into the end of the tube.

'But no,' said the master. 'We need translucence here. Yes.'

He went muttering to the bookcases and drew out a volume. He opened it and Will saw to his amazement a wonderful picture of a horse, drawn so fine and life-like that—

The master ripped out the tissue paper which protected the engraving and put the book back on the shelf. The fine paper was used to line the lens, and then fragments of coloured glass went into the tube and were trapped behind another lens. Then the mirrors were wound round with cotton to form a triangular tunnel which was pushed into the tube after the lenses, and the eyepiece of the telescope was screwed in tight after it.

The master held the thing at last, shifting from foot to foot with excitement, weighing it in his fingers. 'A light,' he muttered. 'We need a bright light. Light a candle, boy, and put it on the desk.'

The master bent his sharp joints into his chair. He put the tube tremblingly to his eye and stared through it at the little dancing flame.

There was a long, long silence. Then the bony fingers twisted and the tube turned. The room was so still that Will heard the tiny clatter of the glass fragments tumbling to a new rest inside the tube.

Will wondered what the master could see. Something wonderful, without a doubt. Something magic, maybe. But could it be anything powerful enough to keep away a whole army of rebels?

Will, confused and afraid, thought of Rosie's creamy face and Miss Winter's straw-coloured hair.

Downstairs the clock struck. Another hour gone, and Will had a hundred other things to do before he could go to his rest.

'Would you be needing me any more, sir?' he asked, at last.

He had to say it twice before the man gave any sign of hearing.

'No,' he said, without taking his eye from the tube. 'It is all here. Beauty and regularity and pattern and infinity. *Kaleidos. Kaleidos. Scopein.*'

'I beg your pardon, sir?' asked Will, bewildered.

The thin lips beneath the tube twitched a little.

'It is a learned tongue,' he said. 'Now go. I am safe, now.'

Red, for blood.

    No.

    Red, for red, that's all. Turning like the spheres, in order.

    Green, for nothing. Excellent. Blue, for eyes that reflect themselves.

Searching, searching. For nothing.

There were shadows on the landing. Will was going to walk through them when one spoke.

'William!'

Will leapt half out of his skin as one of the shadows detached itself from the others and spoke again.

'My brother. How is he? Is he calmer, now?'

'Well—yes, ma'am. He's made himself a tube of colours. A pattern of them, I think. He seems vastly pleased with it, ma'am.'

Miss Winter stepped forward some more and her face appeared, blue-tinged in the fading light.

'Does he still insist that we must stay here with him in the house?'

'Well . . . I don't know as he's changed his mind, ma'am.'

She laughed, suddenly, opening a dark tunnel in the grey-blue of her face. Will found himself shivering.

'No. Of course not. He never changes his mind. Never, since I was born. He has always been caught up in his own ways. Everything has always had to be just so, or he would frighten us with violence. My poor father did what he could to govern him. He hired a doctor, but it did no good. Indeed, the doctor's bindings and punishments made things worse, for they turned my brother even more in on himself. You know, I myself was the best at reaching him; I think my smallness helped. I was the one who understood his genius, too, a little: who recognized it, in any case. Oh, the distress of that time! But still, the doctor's drugs did help. They calmed him, and sometimes it seemed worth it for the sake of peace, but . . . '

The wind shook her skirts, whipping them into grotesque shapes, so she seemed almost a thing of shadows herself, insubstantial.

'We cannot stay here,' said Miss Winter. 'I have been here nearly all my life, but we cannot stay here any longer. My brother is a genius, but he does not understand how people are. I have given my life for him, my whole life, but my life is only a penny-weight and I would be throwing it away to no purpose. We cannot stay here.'

'No, ma'am,' said Will; and his heart suddenly leapt with the thought of *somewhere else*: somewhere further than the village, somewhere further than his eyes had ever seen.

And somehow he felt the same excitement spark in Miss Winter's thin chest.

'It is the only way,' she said, as if she'd made a decision.

'Ma'am?'

She shook herself back to the present.

'We must get on, Will,' she said. 'We must be leaving at first light. Let's get on.'

Chapter 13

Will found Rosie in the pantry. Her face, always pale as cream, was white with tiredness.

'Taking even a pot of jam with us would weigh us down too much,' she said, wearily. 'We are going to have to leave it all behind, Will.'

Will looked at her. That was all he'd wanted to do, really, to look at her. He stood and looked at the way her belly swelled softly under her apron, and the little heels on her boots that showed when she stood on tiptoe to reach to the back of a shelf.

Outside, the dusk had settled into night. Tomorrow, as soon as dawn was breaking, they would be gone. He might never be in this house in clear daylight again.

He'd prop the hen-house door ajar so that perhaps the hens might roost safe from the fox, and Rosie would milk the cow for the last time and turn it free to find someone who would care for it.

The guns were still sounding, occasionally, but they seemed no nearer, and no more horses had come along the road.

'I can carry more,' said Will. 'I will carry anything you like for you.'

She half turned, so that he saw the smudge of shadow under the plumpness of her jaw.

'You'll have enough to do, Will,' she said, too tired even to be affronted. 'It'll all have to be left, that's all. And when I think of the hours I spent standing over the pans, with the sugar bubbling under my nose until my face was as red as the jam was!'

Will remembered her, flushed and tired and triumphant, as at last the little drop of burgundy jam on the saucer went dull, and wrinkled, and set.

'I could carry it all down to the cellar,' he offered, though his back screamed at the thought of lifting anything. 'Or I could dig out a hole and bury it. It'd be safe, then, Rosie, and then perhaps we could come back and get it later on.'

Rosie turned round properly then.

'And haven't you got your own duties to attend to?' she demanded, suddenly impatient. 'Mr Gilfry, he'll be after you, I'll lay. Where is he?'

Out in the barn, still, probably, Will realized, with an awful pang of guilt. Will had quite forgotten him.

'He'll be cold,' went on Rosie, inexorably. 'Stuck in that chair as he is, poor man.'

'I'm sorry,' said Will, in a hot muddle of guilt and inadequacy. 'I'm sorry. I'll go and find him. Rosie!'

'What?'

'I only wanted to help you,' said Will.

She put her hands on her hips (on her *hips*, so that her skirts kicked out at the sides and rode up just a little, so that if he were standing by the door he could have seen her boots, and perhaps a slice of sturdy ankle clung round with stocking . . .)

'You've forgotten yourself,' she said. 'As if *I'd* need you to help me, Will Nunn. I've a family, I have. *And* a sweetheart. *And* I can cook and sew and wait on a lady.'

'I know,' said Will, humbly. 'I know, Rosie.'

Of course he knew all that, of course he did. Rosie was fine and lovely and clever and he—and he was nothing. Almost nothing.

'Rosie!' he said, again, at the door.

'Well?' she demanded.

'Even—even a *donkey* can be useful, sometimes, Rosie.'

She couldn't help smiling.

'Be off with you, then, and be useful, you silly fool,' she said; but she said it without anger.

It was properly dark outside. Mr Gilfry was in his chair, rubbing his great hands together for warmth, his breath steaming like a bull's. He turned his head when he heard Will's coming.

'There you are,' he said. 'And you've been working flat out all day, Will, I'll warrant. I'm sorry to be of so little help to you.'

Will hurried over, filled with shame.

'Can you wheel me inside, now, lad? That's it, that's it.'

Mr Gilfry put out his great arms to help steer the chair through the kitchen door. He even managed to give an extra tug to help get him up and over the threshold, though the jar of the chair hitting the flags on the other side made him grunt.

The golden kitchen smelled of warmth and baking. Mrs Keen came bustling forward, wide with welcome.

'You must be half froze, the pair of you,' she said. 'Come along, come along, there's supper in the pot, and a fine big supper, too, for there's no point in leaving more than we have to for those blackguards that are on their way. Ten to one they'll knock the place to bits with their silly great cannon balls.'

Toby shook his head tragically as he dunked a hunk of bread into the rich brownness of his stew.

'I know how you feel, Mrs Keen,' he said. 'Torn, I am. It'd be death not to get well out of the way of this thieving, murdering lot, and I'd have been well away hours ago if I'd dared set out alone; but I have to say my heart's against it. I mean, I've settled down the dunghill as best I can, but I'm not easy in my mind about it, not by a long chalk.'

'Aye,' said Mr Gilfry. 'And we can't help but leave a parcel of timber behind, and the cross-cut saw, too.'

Mrs Keen compressed her mouth into a determined line.

'Well, we must bear up as cheerfully as we can,' she said. 'Our brave boys'll be more than a match for that rabble in the end, you may be sure of that. And we must remember that there's worse that can happen than having to move house, after all.'

Toby grunted.

'That's true enough,' he said.

In the angry dusk the remains of the battle lay black on the churned mud. And the place was quieter than a victory should have been. Lonelier. And I, the warrior, was afraid.

I raised one fist to the sky in token of my triumph, and then I began to search for my friends.

Chapter 14

Deep cold set in during the night, a hard white frost that chilled them all to furtive dashes through the shadowy house. Everywhere there were signs that they would soon be gone. The plates at breakfast were the oldest, oddest plates; the meal, though extra-large and nourishing, was not the usual meal.

'I don't suppose there's much point in scouring the pans,' said Mrs Keen, getting fatly to her feet, 'but there, I won't rest if I don't do it.'

'Sam, clean your face,' said Rosie. 'I'm not going to be seen out in company with you, we'll be taken for a pack of gypsies.'

Sam went to wipe his mouth on his sleeve, caught Rosie's eye, and thought better of it.

'The water's frozen in the trough,' he said, but without real hope.

'Then break it.'

'And then we must be bringing the horses out,' said Toby, getting ponderously up. 'So hurry up with you, young Sam.'

'Now where's the master's tray?' asked Mrs Keen, turning round in a circle. 'I'm sure I put it on the side.'

'Miss Winter took it, Mrs Keen,' said Rosie.

'Miss Winter?' Mrs Keen looked surprised. 'Well, I suppose she's trying to make the master comfortable on his last morning. I don't envy her the task of persuading him to leave the house, poor girl. Why, he's hardly seen the sun these twenty years. Still, there's no helping it for any of us. Did you fill the green teapot for her?'

'Yes, Mrs Keen. And I put seven pieces of sugar in the bowl, all triangular ones, just as the master likes, and three and one half spoonfuls of pudding in one of the blue-rimmed bowls.'

'Good girl. That should do him, then.'

'Will!'

'Yes, Mr Gilfry?'

'Time I was in the driving seat.'

Will had worked out a way for Mr Gilfry to drive the horses from the bath chair, but he'd not given any thought to how they would get Mr Gilfry up onto the wagon. It took a lot of undignified heaving and shoving. It was lucky that Sam was there: his glee took away some of the grim embarrassment of Mr Gilfry's humiliation, and his huzzahs when Mr Gilfry was finally ensconced lifted all their hearts.

The horses had not been in harness since harvest, and they were nervous—spooked by the archway, and unsettled by the noise of their hooves on the frost-grey cobbles.

'They should be shod, really,' said Sam, stroking their bronze noses to reassure them. 'Especially with the road set hard in this frost.'

'It's only a day's journey, Sam,' said Mr Gilfry. 'You must be sure to pick out their hooves whenever you get the chance, and apart from that we must hope for the best.'

There were a hundred things Will hadn't done. He knew it, deep in his chilly bones, though he couldn't remember what they were. In the small amount of sleep he'd snatched during the night he'd dreamed of them: sometimes he even remembered one or two of them for a moment; but by the time he'd finished answering everybody's questions, or following everybody's orders, then he'd always forgotten them again.

'Will!'

'Yes, Mr Gilfry?' said Will, running in circles. 'Yes, Sam? Yes, Mrs Keen?'

But at last Will looked round the courtyard and found that people were beginning to gather, stamping against the cold and blowing hard onto their fingers.

'William!'

And here was Miss Winter coming up, much too close, so he could smell the camphor that had been protecting the ancient fur on her cuffs.

'I need your help,' she said, whiter even than usual. 'The master . . . I fear the master is unwell. Come with me.'

She hurried ahead of him, into the house and past the door of the abandoned Great Hall, talking rapidly all the time.

'The master's mind is bound up in his experiments, in this new kaleidoscope. I know it is my duty to see that he can work in peace, but he does not understand what is happening.'

Miss Winter came to the top of the stair-mountain and turned left towards the family's rooms.

'Quickly, William. We have left him too long.'

Will followed her, treading gingerly. This was territory as foreign to him as the tower. It smelt of cedarwood and stale air.

Miss Winter paused by a door, took a gasping, nervous breath, and turned the brass handle.

It was dim inside, for the curtains were still drawn, but on a chair in front of the window was a large awkward bundle. All Will could make out was a pale thing like a skull that hung on the top of it.

And then he looked again and he found that it *was* a skull . . . or very nearly.

For a moment Will thought the master was dead. He must certainly be dying, for his head was dragging forward, swaying on its neck as though the sharp nose weighed it down, and the eyes, the sharp black eyes, were as dull and dead as coals.

The numbness of Will's fingers and feet swept right through him in a rush of horror.

Miss Winter pattered thinly to her brother's side.

'We are ready, now, Arthur,' she said. 'It is time to go.'

She put a hand on his arm, but at her touch his whole body went into a spasm, jerking and twisting and falling sideways in the chair. Miss Winter tried to catch him, to save him, but he was all flailing lashing limbs like a giant spider and she had no chance.

Will didn't run away. He wanted to, sure enough, for he was as scared as he had ever been, but the master was hitting Miss Winter with vicious random arms. So he went to help her.

The master was near death, Will felt certain, and in agony, too. His back was bucking and twisting with such violence that Miss Winter had not the strength to restrain him. He slipped down onto the polished floorboards, and there was coming from him, nightmarishly, a dreadful high whine like an injured dog.

But then some energy seemed to desert him, for he stopped struggling. He was only twitching faintly, now, still not quite dead, but surely in terrible pain, for the whining was going on and on until Will wanted more than anything for the master to die, now, and be out of his misery.

'Help me with him,' said Miss Winter, breathlessly.

The master's eyes were showing yellow crescents like old nail clippings, and there was a dribble of bronze at the corner of his mouth.

Will did not want to touch him.

'Come, we must get him down to the wagon. Take his arm, William. Take care, for his bones are not strong.'

The master's limbs now hung lifelessly, and Will wanted more than ever to run away.

'The apothecary has already left the village, ma'am,' he said, uneasily.

'He does not need one. He has had this malady before, when he was a boy. It is not serious—at least,

84

he will recover. I have drops which I shall give him from time to time. His mind has withdrawn, that's all. It is the shock of having to leave the house that has caused it, without a doubt.'

The master was a small man, all stunted bones and dry flesh, or they could not have managed him. They lifted him, with his sweat-stained armpits spreading warmth to their necks, and stumbled down the draughty stairs. Will was half a head taller than Miss Winter, and much stronger, but she managed as best she could and made no complaint.

The master flinched as the light of the courtyard hit him and he began to lash out again, to howl, and they would have dropped him if Toby and Mrs Keen had not come to their aid.

'His reason is quite overturned, poor soul,' puffed Mrs Keen, ducking a wild blow that might have had her bonnet off. 'What a thing to happen at this moment!'

Toby got a nasty hack on the shins and had to limp round in an agonized circle before he could trust himself to say anything.

'He's completely crazed,' he said, at last. 'Hadn't we better take that metal tube away from him? He could do real damage with that.'

But the master fought and howled so piteously that they could not bear to do it.

'It's his kaleidoscope,' explained Will, at last. 'Whatever you look at, it becomes quite beautiful, and not like things really are. It keeps the soldiers away, he says.'

'Does it?' said Toby, quickly. 'Best let him keep it, then. You never know what may be out there, after all.'

'Yes, let him keep it,' said Miss Winter. 'It may give him comfort. He sees horrors all around. He is in terror of the outside, of strangers.'

'And he's not alone,' said Mrs Keen, with a shudder. 'Oh, but poor soul, poor soul.'

Mr Gilfry frowned.

'But so has he always been afraid,' he said. 'There must be more to this than that accounts for. Something must have happened to reduce him to this so suddenly.'

'There was no other way—' began Miss Winter: and stopped.

Mr Gilfry cleared his throat into the sudden silence.

'The master can sit beside me,' he said. 'Will, you must find some cords to secure him, or he is like to throw himself off onto the road.'

It wasn't easy to get the master onto the wagon, even with everybody's help. One minute he would hang limply in their arms, and the next he would be flailing about so wildly that they only just prevented him from plunging head first onto the cobbles. And he kept making noises—little groans, and mutterings, and an awful repeated whine like a whipped hound.

Will got down from the wagon at last, ruffled, and heated, and feeling soiled.

Miss Winter stood herself straight, and looked

all round. Her bonnet had been bashed sideways, but she stood as tall as she could. And there was a new light in her eye: an excitement, a simmering determination, perhaps even a hope.

'Are we all ready, now?'

'Aye, ma'am,' said Rosie. She looked serious, but she was eager, too. Toby's answer was to start walking.

'As near as we will be, ma'am,' agreed Mr Gilfry, arranging the reins between his thick fingers.

'Then we'll be on our way.'

Keep away. Keep away, or I will kill you!

But help me. She has dragged me down into a spinning storm and I am drowning. I cannot see, cannot see, and my body has been stolen by . . .

Red and blue and hot and ice and close close close close close.

Help me.

Chapter 15

Will knew the road to the village, though he did not walk it often. Until this morning his place had been in the barn: and now he had no place at all.

The deserted almshouse stood back a little from the road. Its front garden was filled with rows of pale cold cabbages and sticks marking the lines where next year's dinners would grow. Will had worked there picking stones from the time he could walk. It was impossible to imagine soldiers here.

The frost, alighting fiercely in the night, had frozen the mud to a powderiness that was almost like summer's, though the air cut sharply into their lungs. The wagon trundled along, six inches deep in the ruts, and Will walked along beside the great wheels, watching the grey ash of the felloes turning round the biscuit-coloured elm of the hubs. If one of the wheels failed then they were all as stranded as a felled tree, for there would be no hope of shifting the great blue wagon ever again.

They had been fools to load the wagon so heavily. Will had known that, even while he was doing it.

Will looked back along the line of people, which was already beginning to straggle. Mrs Keen was strong and fat, but she was not used to walking, and Toby was so deep in worrying gloom that his chin hung halfway to his belly-button. Rosie was re-settling her pack on her shoulders. Will was sure she was carrying more than she should, but he didn't dare offer to help her again. At the rear came Miss Winter. The master's illness had affected her, but oddly, for she was looking round at the scarlet and lemon and gold of the trees as if she were searching for something; and she seemed more alive, more excited, even, than he had ever seen her. It seemed strange when her brother was taken so ill and they were travelling with danger at their heels. Will did not understand it.

He looked round again and spotted Sam, who had pulled himself up behind the blue wagon to hitch a lift.

'Hey, Sam,' said Will, his mind pulled back to the groaning axles and the stripes of rot in the floor planks. 'Don't you know we're over-loaded?'

'I won't make much difference,' said Sam.

'Even a penny might make the difference,' said Will. 'You come down, now!'

But Sam climbed neatly right up to the top of the load.

'You're like an old hen with one chick, you are, Will, you and this blooming wagon.'

And then, while Will was wondering whether he should fetch Sam down and deliver him to Rosie, Sam's attention was caught by something ahead along the road.

'Mr Gilfry!' he said, suddenly urgent. 'There's people over there! By those bushes!'

'Whoa, there!' said Mr Gilfry, as he pulled the horses up.

They drew together like a flock of sheep.

'People? What sort of people?' asked Toby, poised for flight.

'Will, can you see?' asked Mr Gilfry.

Will hauled himself up beside Sam, feeling the weight of his pack dragging him back as he did.

'I can see two horses, Mr Gilfry,' he said. 'Well, one's a pony, maybe.'

Mrs Keen brought down her carpet-beater from her shoulder and held it ready in both hands.

'But friend or foe?' she asked, grimly.

Mr Gilfry hesitated.

'Can you see nothing else, Will?' he asked.

'I can, I can!' yelped Sam. 'I can see a scarlet coat. One's a soldier, sure enough!'

A soldier: but a scarlet soldier, a King's man. Will, standing high above the little colourful people, saw them relax a little. He helped Sam down from the load, and Mr Gilfry touched the horses back into motion. The people ahead were invisible from the ground to begin with, but soon Will could see shapes flickering through the thousand slender switches of the hazel coppice that lined the bend; and then the horses came into sight.

Will had been right, there were two horses, both riderless. One was a yellow dun pony, and the other—oh, the other was magnificent. And when a tall man who must be its rider stepped out from behind some bushes, mounted, and turned his horse to meet them. Will suddenly was washed with giddiness, as if he was seeing a vision.

Scarlet and white, the man was, with boots varnished like molten pitch, and he'd a shining helmet stamped with a crown, with a cockade on top to make him sit even taller.

The soldier rode along the road towards them, with his servant boy riding a humble few paces behind him.

And Will felt as if the King himself had come amongst them.

Chapter 16

The soldier raised a white-gloved hand in greeting.

'Good morning to you,' he called. 'Where are you headed?'

Mr Gilfry raised his hat respectfully. Will found himself standing open-mouthed, hardly able to breathe for the splendour before him.

'Along to my master's other house, Captain,' said Mr Gilfry. 'The Red House, it is called. We heard as there was likely to be fighting around here, so we decided we'd best get out of the way of it.'

The man nodded, and the stamped crown on his helmet flashed in the sun, which had edged shyly out of the morning mist to do him homage. The man had white teeth and blue eyes and a fine hooked nose and Will was overtaken by a huge need to serve him. At that moment he would have died for him, and felt grateful for the chance.

'That's wise, without a doubt,' the captain said. 'Is your master and his family gone ahead of you?'

'No, sir. The master is taken sadly ill, as you can see. But here is the mistress.'

Miss Winter was standing by one of the great wheels of the wagon. Will glanced back at her—and then he looked again. She was gawping, if anything, even more foolishly than Sam was; but something had happened to her. She had become—it was ridiculous—but her grey skin had flushed pink, and she was suddenly, well, plumper. Younger. Almost *young*.

The captain bowed in his saddle.

'I'm sorry to see you on such a sad errand, ma'am, and at such an uncertain time.'

Miss Winter swallowed hard, as if trying to settle some of her wits back into place.

'Are . . . are the rebels still advancing, Captain?' she asked.

'We can't be sure of that, ma'am, but they will certainly have sent scouting parties into the area, and I doubt we'll intercept them all.' He frowned, and ran his eyes over the great tied-down load that was threatening to burst the raves of the wagon apart. 'And you would hardly out-run a hand-cart, loaded up as you are.'

'I'm afraid that's true,' agreed Miss Winter; but then she smiled, quite suddenly, and Will was nearly as startled as if Mr Gilfry's old apron had got up by itself and begun to dance a jig. 'But we've done what we can to keep things safe,' she went on. 'The most valuable things, the jewellery and the money and the silver, are not on the wagon at all.'

The man surveyed them all. Will stood up as tall as he could. Rosie smiled nearly as widely as the mistress, and even Toby put his spade smartly over his shoulder.

'Well,' said the captain seriously. 'Our paths lie together for a while, and I shall do what I can to see you safely on your way. Is there anything my servant may carry for you? His pony will make light work of your burdens.'

The captain's own horse was weighed down already, what with its haynet and oatbag, and the carbine and broadsword. Will kept closing his mouth, only for it to fall open again in wonder at all the splendour in front of him. It wasn't until he caught sight of Sam, who was gawping like a stranded trout, that he managed to pull himself together.

'That is so very kind,' began Miss Winter; but Mrs Keen spoke up quite sharply, a sour note amongst all the cooing.

'Thank you kindly, sir, but I'm sure we'll manage our burdens quite as well as your boy, there. I'm short of wind, I admit, but I'm strong, sure enough. You would not find many as would put money on him in a fight between him and me, I'm sure.'

The captain laughed out loud. It seemed a long time since anyone had laughed properly. It gave them a new energy. Why, Miss Winter even laughed herself, though it was a strange unpractised effort like the squeal of an ungreased saw.

'It will be a great comfort to have your company, Captain,' she said earnestly.

'But it will be of most comfort to be safely at your destination, ma'am,' said the captain. 'For I'm afraid you are all far from safety here.'

The company had straggled along the road

before, but now they walked bunched together around the captain, drawn to him like nails to a magnet. Even Mrs Keen, no admirer of a red coat since Mr Keen had been taken from her, lumbered along beside them as best she could. Will, with something else to think about, stopped watching the wagon wheels turning ponderously round. He even stopped worrying about the worn nail-heads on the strakes.

'My brother is unwell, as you can see,' Miss Winter was telling the captain. 'He was taken with a violent fit just this morning, but of course we had no choice but to set out.'

'Indeed not, ma'am.'

Mrs Keen heaved a sigh.

'This war is a terrible thing,' she said. 'Why, my own dear husband has been obliged to leave me to join the fighting. Captain, if I might make so bold, sir, have you come across a Trooper Keen at any time?'

'Or a Gilfry, sir?' asked Mr Gilfry, from his high seat. 'A strong, dark, well-set-up youngster, with a scar across his left hand?'

But the captain shook his head.

'I wish I could give you news of them,' he said, 'but there are now many thousands of men fighting for the cause.'

Will found himself swept with longing. *Fighting for the cause.* Oh, but to be part of such a glorious, splendid thing was surely not terrible at all, but hugely, overwhelmingly marvellous.

Astonishingly Miss Winter seemed to feel something of the same fervency, for she was saying:

'We rely on the best and finest to fight for us, Captain.'

Mrs Keen sighed even more heavily.

'That's true, ma'am. And when I think of those raping, murdering savages I'm sure I do not know whether to hope for a great bloody battle or not. It is all a terrible, terrible puzzle and it makes my head spin.'

But Will's heart was thumping at the thought of battle. He imagined himself, fine and scarlet, with a musket in his hand. Just suppose if the captain were to ask him to tag along—oh, with what a hop and a skip and a jump he'd go.

'A war requires great sacrifices of us all,' agreed Miss Winter. She seemed determined to keep smiling, though Will could never recall her smiling before. It quite transformed her. He even found himself wondering if an elderly man, with failing sight, perhaps, might find her interesting . . . but then he shuddered away from that bizarre thought.

'You yourself, Captain,' Miss Winter went on, 'must have left many loved ones at home.'

A look of alarm seemed to pass across the captain's face; but that could only have been an effect of the blue flickering shadows of the trees, for surely such a man could never be afraid of anything.

'Well, no, ma'am,' he admitted, uneasily. 'No one in particular.'

'I am glad of it,' said Miss Winter, with great sincerity. And she did indeed look extremely joyful at the news. 'It must save you much anxiety.'

Toby grunted.

'Not that we can all help but be filled with anxiety,' he said. 'What with danger along every road and round every corner. It cannot help but affect us, mind and body, nerves and digestion. And there's no end to the damage a deranged set of bowels can cause. Why, I've seen a whole row of carrots attacked by fly after an inappropriate application. Tragic, it can be.'

The captain's boy was leading his fat yellow pony along the grass by the roadside. He was half a head shorter than Will, and could be no older, but Will was filled with huge respect for him. This boy would have seen battles, perhaps, and ambushes and skirmishes—great men and great deeds—ranks of scarlet, marching, shooting, fighting. And this boy would have helped them, perhaps. Have served the captain. Been necessary to him.

The wagon was drawing level now with the place where Sam had first spotted the captain, and it was only because Will's mind was full of fighting scarlet coats that he registered a glimpse of something else scarlet behind the purple spikes of a blackthorn bush.

Something scarlet, lying amongst the scrubby grass and spikes of rusty dock.

Will's feet stopped walking.

The others has not seen it: they were all clustered round the captain for one thing, and anyway, the captain's boy was shielding it from their view. Yes, that was why he was walking his pony through the long grass, even though it powdered him to the calves with frost.

But Will had seen. Had half seen. He took two more steps towards it.

He looked at it carefully until he could make sense of it. He was used to people having their skin whole, and their insides inside. But this man . . .

Will looked away and the cold air stung his eyes. The others were going past. Toby was stomping along chewing dourly at a windlestraw, and Mrs Keen was rolling along humming to herself. Miss Winter, still strangely excited, was chattering at the captain.

The yellow dun pony had stopped beside him.

'How did this happen?' Will asked, trying not to sound too shaken.

'How should I know?' said the captain's boy, a little defensively. 'He was dead when we found him, wasn't he.'

Will felt his eyes drawn back to the scarlet coat, and the waistcoat that had once been white, but which now so nearly and horribly matched it.

The face was an ordinary face. A face you might see any day. The man's left hand . . .

Will leant over to look, was caught by the stink of the blood, and stood up quickly, sickened.

The man's left hand had a finger missing. The flesh was raw where it had been cut off.

I cannot say how terrible it was to search the battlefield, and fear what I would find. It made

me realize what was important. Who was important. I found one important man. He had been cut in two. I wept, for part of me had died with him, but I carried on my search.

'He would have been wearing a ring,' the captain's boy explained, off-handedly, from somewhere far away. 'Someone has gone through his clothes, too, looking for his watch, or a seal, or a locket with the hair of a loved one inside. That's fashionable at the moment. And money, of course.'

Will turned his back on the corpse and took in a deep breath of untainted air.

'You were shielding us from seeing this,' he said.

The captain's boy made a small encouraging noise to his pony, and its warm body stepped delicately forward onto the road after the others.

'Of course I was,' he said. 'It's not something anyone would wish to see. It would frighten the ladies.'

Will glanced back at the body, but only a lonely boot was visible, now.

'Shouldn't we bury him?'

'In this frozen ground? It's not our concern, in any case.'

Will stumbled along feeling ill in his stomach. A *glorious death*, he told himself—and tried not to be reminded of the butcher's shop.

'Are you all right?'

Will took in another deep breath.

'Yes. Yes. Thank you kindly.'

The captain's boy gave him a sideways, assessing glance.

'It is a shock, at first,' he said.

Will forced a smile.

'I've never been far from home,' he said. 'And I know I'm sadly ignorant. But you will have seen many such sights before.'

The captain's boy shrugged.

There is air here. So now I can breathe. But where am I?

Not safe. Not safe. Not safe.

But my mind is still alive, and I shall find it, in time. They have not caught it yet, oh no.

Breathe. Breathe . . .

. . . what if the air is poisoned?

Chapter 17

They stopped for bread and carrots and cake at noon. They were all tired from walking, or from matching their pace to that of the wagon. There was a tree stump big enough and dry enough for the women to sit on. Sam filled the carthorses' nose bags and pulled grass for them from the verges. The captain's boy fed the saddle horses from their fodder nets and the men stood around and chewed.

'Take everyone's packs and stow them behind the hedge while we eat,' said the captain to his boy. 'That will be safest.'

'No, I shall do it,' said the captain's boy, when Will went to help. 'We must obey orders.'

And Will retreated, ashamed.

The sun had come through strongly, now, but the ground still struck toe-numbingly cold through the leather of their boots. The tree stump must have been cold, too, for the women soon got up and shook the crumbs out of their skirts. Miss Winter tried to offer food to the master: but he cringed away and would not take even water from his own cup.

'He seems in terror of the water,' said the captain, frowning. 'He has not been bitten by a dog recently?'

'Oh no. No, Captain,' Miss Winter assured him. 'This illness is a result of the fit he had this morning. It is a mysterious ailment, for no one else in the family has ever been affected. And I myself have always enjoyed very good health.'

'It is sad to see such suffering, ma'am. And you say he is normally sound in mind.'

Miss Winter blushed a little, but didn't stop smiling.

'Oh, yes, Captain. Yes, indeed. My brother is a great thinker, a philosopher. He generally leads a very retired life, and I keep house for him. He has a good income, but he believes that regularity is the surest route to peace and security. Why, this device, this tube he clutches, is an invention of his which gives the illusion of peace and order, even when surrounded by the greatest chaos.'

The captain rubbed a thoughtful finger along his jaw.

'Given my profession, you can hardly expect me to appreciate too highly the benefits of peace,' he said. 'And, in any case, security is too much like prison. I think I would rather chance the chaos, ma'am, for good or ill.'

Miss Winter looked him straight in the face and there was something strangely formidable about her; something zealous, almost reckless.

'You are right,' she said. 'Yes, you are certainly right. I, too, am determined to let no chance pass by me, Captain, without grasping it with both hands.'

There was not enough comfort in the place to stay long.

'My pack's got even heavier,' groaned Toby, hoisting it. 'I'll be two inches shorter by this evening, you mark my words. *And* with a cracked spine, as well.'

'You know,' said Mrs Keen, in some surprise, 'mine feels lighter, somehow.'

'And so does mine,' said Rosie. 'There, that exercise this morning must have done us good.'

'Aye, except that it has rusted my poor joints almost solid.'

Mr Gilfry touched the horses into motion and the wagon squealed and trundled on its way. Miss Winter, flushed with cold and urgency, chattered constantly to the captain. Sam kept making faces behind her back, and Rosie was inclined to roll her eyes, but Will could not blame the mistress. The captain was so very fine a man, after all, and if he accepted the invitation Miss Winter was giving him to stay at the Red House then Will, for one, would be more than glad. Why, Will would feel honoured to take breath under the same roof.

'I'm sure such a visit would be a great pleasure, ma'am,' the captain was saying, carefully.

Miss Winter's face flared with happiness. Or triumph, perhaps.

'Then we shall hold you to your promise,' she said; though Will, with his slow wits, had altogether missed the making of a promise.

They had gone on another mile, and the great horses were patiently pulling the wagon round a shallow bend, when the captain suddenly held up a white hand for silence. Mr Gilfry reined in the horses and even Miss Winter let her nervous chatter rest. They all listened. It was hard to hear, for beside them an ash tree was shedding every one of its green leaves. They twirled and fell sullenly, frost-plucked, to the ground.

But there was no doubt about it: there was a trundling of hooves on the road behind them.

'Horsemen,' said Mr Gilfry. 'A fair number of them, by the sound of it. Too many to be ordinary travellers.'

'Soldiers?' asked Toby; and even his pimples turned white.

'Likely enough,' said the captain, grimly, kicking his horse into a trot, 'and rebels, quite likely, too. All away, all away!' he called. 'Leave the wagon! All away behind the wall!'

He was urging the horse forward as he spoke, and the horse was jumping the low flint wall that edged the road, and, almost miraculously, vanishing from sight.

And now the captain's boy was pulling his pony round and making after him.

'Quickly!' he snapped.

And before anyone else could take breath he and the pony had bounded neatly after the captain.

'Over the wall!' Mr Gilfry barked—and the sound of his voice struck them all with haste. Will, his mind filled with a vision of that butchered soldier, pushed Sam towards the wall and then turned to help the women. Rosie had picked up her skirts and was running like a boy, but Miss Winter was still standing dumbstruck, staring at the piece of air that had last contained the captain. Will put his arm through hers and hurried her over to the side of the road. She came, but not fast enough: she kept half twisting back to look at the wagon and tripping over her own feet. And even when they got to the wall she still seemed too distracted to know what to do, so Will picked her up by the skinny middle, swung her with a heave up onto the top of the wall, and only just had presence of mind not to give her a swift push to get her out of sight.

Will looked round. Mrs Keen had a heavy knee up on the wall, and Rosie was there to help her. Toby was jumping down out of sight. Everyone else was hidden except . . .

Will threw himself back across the frozen earth to the wagon. Mr Gilfry was sitting in his bath chair—how could he be otherwise?—and beside him was the slumped twiggy bundle that was the master.

'Get back, Will, get back!' ordered Mr Gilfry. 'Never mind us. We shall manage all right. Be off with you!'

Will grabbed hold of the side of the wagon and heaved himself up. He heaved too hard and landed sprawled across Mr Gilfry's lap, but he wriggled and tumbled into a heap between him and the angular pile of bones that was the master.

'I said be off with you, Will, you young fool! You can't help us!'

Will stood up and looked back in urgent fear. There was a jogging line of darkness showing far back along the road, now. Darkness with a hint of green about it.

'They're rebels, Mr Gilfry,' gasped Will, and he was gripped by a terror that took away all the power from his mind and limbs.

It was too late for Will to run, now. There were black hats bobbing majestically round the corner. Twenty blank-faced men on horseback, green and dark, trotting down the road.

Will's knees gave way. He crouched down so that the mound of the wagon's load hid him from view.

'A tarpaulin, Will,' gasped Mr Gilfry, suddenly. 'Pull a tarpaulin across us. Quick, Will. Quick!'

Will turned, grabbed at the nearest edge of the nearest tarpaulin, and yanked at it with all his strength. It gave a little, rasped out of the knots holding it, and suddenly it was free, smelling of tar and nearly as stiff as a board in the cold air. Mr Gilfry pulled it over the three of them—two quick tugs, and the soldiers only fifty yards away.

'Keep still, now,' growled Mr Gilfry, putting a heavy warm hand on Will's shoulder.

Will panted cautiously into the gloom. Every breath warmed the air, and Will found himself enveloped by the familiar smell of shavings and ale and authority that Mr Gilfry carried with him.

The hooves were hollow on the frozen mud. Will had a strong, strong wish to look out at the soldiers. They'd be large and wicked and full of dreadful purpose: rebels, and the enemy, who burned down towns and killed babies. Ate them, too, or so he'd heard. Killed soldiers and cut off their rings and left the bodies to rot by the side of the road.

The tarpaulin jutted out in a stiff fold by his side: and there, there, in front of Will's eyes, was a shining boot in a steel stirrup—and a groomed-to-gleaming flank—and a plump docked brush of a chestnut tail.

Mr Gilfry's hand tightened on Will's shoulder. Will lay on his stomach and blinked at the dizzying succession of steel and horse and leather. Something, perhaps a spur, scraped the side of the wagon for a moment, and the carthorses plunged their heads until their harness jingled.

And then Will was staring at a momentary patch of ice-dry road; and soon after that the thudding of the hooves was all in front of them; and then he heard again a muffled *thump* which was some far-away gun, audible again now the horses were past them.

Will took a deep breath and discovered that his ear was squashed painfully against something. He moved a little and discovered it was the master's knee. And now Mr Gilfry was pushing the tarpaulin away, and there by the side of the road was a hazel tree hung with pink stiff catkins and leaves like a thousand golden guineas.

Will sat up, gave his ear a rub, and took the sharp cold air into his lungs.

'I hope the knots you used to tie the load down are better than the ones you used on the tarpaulin,' said Mr Gilfry, drily.

Will looked back over the mound of the load and hoped so, too.

'I get my left and right mixed up, sometimes, Mr Gilfry,' he admitted.

Mr Gilfry regarded him with faded blue eyes.

'We'll have to tie a string round one of your wrists, Will,' he said. 'That'll soon get that sorted out.'

All along the flint wall heads were popping up. It reminded Will of the Punch and Judy man, and he suddenly, stupidly, wanted to laugh. He picked his way round Mr Gilfry's massive frame so he could jump down.

'Will!' said Mr Gilfry.

'Yes, Mr Gilfry?'

'You acted foolishly, to come back to help us.'

Will said nothing, for there was nothing to say. What was a fool to do, except be foolish? But he was glad to have seen the soldiers so close—though, to be sure, it was surprising that such black-hearted men should be so fine and smart. He wondered if George wore such fine boots.

'Well, get on, boy,' said Mr Gilfry. 'Get on.'

Miss Winter had gone a little way across the field to look out for the captain, but Will helped the others clamber back onto the road.

'That was brave, Will,' said Rosie, seriously.

'Just foolish,' Will told her; but suddenly he was happier than he had ever been.

Mrs Keen began to laugh.

'And I thought myself too fat to run!' she said. 'What a sight we must have looked, indeed.'

'And where is the captain and his precious boy?' asked Toby, sourly, pulling thorns from his hands from where he'd jumped over the wall into a bramble. 'They soon showed us their heels when there was a sign of danger, didn't they?'

Will helped Miss Winter back over the wall when at last it was clear even to her that the captain was not returning immediately. She still blinked around, though, as if expecting to find him coming down the road.

'Perhaps the captain's horse took fright,' she said, wrinkling her brow. 'Or perhaps he has some plan he had not time to convey to us.'

'Aye,' said Toby. 'And if I'd had a horse, I'd have had the same plan, at that!'

And he trundled away, picking wincingly at his skin.

Mr Gilfry gathered up the reins.

'The captain will know where to find us, ma'am, if he so wishes,' he said, and clicked his tongue at the horses.

'Yes,' said Miss Winter, brightening, 'and he is very concerned about us. And he promised to visit. Yes, he knows where we were headed.'

'Will,' asked Sam, quietly, when the wagon had gathered itself into creaking motion again, 'will we meet more soldiers, do you think? More rebels?'

'I don't know, Sam,' said Will. 'I'm afraid we might. But they'll all be busy. I doubt they'll have time to bother too much with someone as small as you.'

'But you aren't small, Will,' said Sam. 'When you went to help Mr Gilfry and the master—weren't you afraid the soldiers would shoot you, or run you through? Or cut you up and eat you? They all had swords, for I peered over the wall and saw them.'

'I was in too much of a hurry and a muddle to think about it, much, Sam.'

Sam walked along for a little while. Then he said:

'Everyone else was in a hurry to run away. Even the captain.'

'Well, you see, Sam, the captain is a soldier. He has other duties besides looking after us. He must be sure to get back to his general to help with the fighting. And it'll be his boy's duty to follow the captain.'

They walked on some more.

'Working with the horses is a trade, isn't it?' said Sam, at last. 'Like being a carpenter. It's sort of the same.'

'Of course it is. A very important trade indeed,' said Will; and Sam, satisfied, ran off to walk by the horses' heads.

I found him in the end. The last important one. I saw his hair, dark as ebony, and his fingers, beseeching in the mud, and I felt the chill of death sweep over me. I ran to him. I even, hopeless, called his name.

And he heard me.

He opened his eyes—and then the glory of our victory swept me up. We had come past death. And we were bound, all of our company, into one.

Chapter 18

Will had checked the wagon over before they'd set off: some of the floor planks were rotten, and several of the strakes were so loose that the many joints of the wheels moved and creaked and threatened to come adrift. He'd hammered everything together, but the nail heads were worn nearly through, so that didn't help much. Once the wagon was in motion things were even more alarming, for it made a whole selection of noises as it went along, all deeply worrying. There was a squeal like a scorched piglet, a whole haunting of groans, and so many rattles and squawks that Will was sure he was listening to the wagon shaking itself to bits. How the master could sleep through the noise he didn't know, but sleep he did, all afternoon, like one drugged.

'For myself, I'm surprised the wagon's gone on as long as it has,' said Toby, mournfully.

The wheels weren't on straight on the axles, either: they leaned out horribly at the tops as they turned.

'Look out!' snapped Rosie, as Will, trying to work out why the wheels were so far out of true, very nearly allowed the off back wheel to run over his foot.

'You great ninny,' she went on. 'A fine mess the rest of us would be in if you go and crock yourself. You'd get your foot crushed to splinters, you would, what with the ground being so hard.'

Will blushed crimson with shame and fell over his feet.

'All cartwheels turn on the slant like that, anyway,' said Rosie. 'Have you never *looked* at a cartwheel before?'

'I don't know,' said Will. 'I suppose not, then.'

Rosie rolled her eyes to the sky.

'I wonder you have the sense in your fat head to keep breathing,' she said. 'Here we are, with a chance to see a bit of the world for once. One short day, between being buried in one house and smothered in another. And you spend all your time fretting and worrying with your nose covered in axle-grease.'

'I'm sorry,' said Will, wiping his nose on his sleeve and making the effort to look around him. Below the blue-wisped sky there were nervous busy birds foraging in the treetops, gorging themselves before the famine of winter. 'But, Rosie,' he went on, 'if the wagon fails—'

'I just hope the Red House has fuel aplenty,' said Rosie. 'This cold is enough for us all to catch our deaths. I'm sure I'm covered from head to foot in goosebumps.'

'I think it's going to turn warmer,' said Will, steering his mind away from all those goosebumps; for although beside the road the dry sticks of the elder were patched with scabs of frozen lichen, the grass was beginning to shiver in a wicked little breeze. 'I hope we don't get bogged down in the mud,' he went on. 'Though if the road is softer, it will jolt the wagon less, to be sure.'

Rosie heaved a huge sigh.

'You are the greatest dim-wit I have ever heard tell of,' she said, witheringly. 'Compared with you even the master has sense and brains!'

Will was deeply startled and shocked. Rosie was beyond doubt one of the cleverest, most beautiful people in the whole world; but what she had just said was so wicked he could hardly credit what he was hearing. He swallowed hard and scanned the sky fearfully for thunderbolts.

None came.

'Of course I am, compared with the master,' he said. 'Of course I am. Why, he's an educated gentleman and has read books and all.'

Rosie snorted.

'Oh yes, books full of numbers and the stars in the sky. But there's nothing there of any use. I never heard tell of a book that was any use. Unless it might be a recipe book, I suppose.'

Will thought of all those brown volumes stuffed full of words, so tantalizingly beyond his reach for ever.

'I do not know what is in books,' he said wistfully. 'But I should like to know, all the same. It would be a fine thing, to know things.'

'Oh yes?' said Rosie, with scorn. 'Why, with

your weak head a single tale might overturn your brain, Will Nunn, and that's for certain.'

A shiver of excitement ran through Will.

'Are there tales in books?' he asked.

Rosie shrugged.

'Aye. Sometimes. Foolish tales of loves and hatreds. Fairy tales.'

'And fighting, Rosie? Are there tales of battles and soldiers?'

'I daresay.'

Will tried to imagine how a tale, a living, breathing thing, could be trapped and preserved between the covers of a book. It might be a little like the flowers that Miss Winter had pressed in the summer, or the cases of stiff butterflies on the landing wall.

'I wish I could make a book out,' said Will. 'I know I'd never do it, of course, because I'm too stupid, but I should like to full well. Why, it would—it would give me a window on the world,' he finished up, longingly.

'No it wouldn't,' snapped Rosie. 'For you would not be able to judge what was right in it. Some of those books, they say all sorts of nonsense. Why, some of them, they would have a young lady give up everything, just for love. They do not mention the advantages of a regular income and a position in life. They do not mention the inconvenience of starving. They are nothing but rubbish, most of them.'

Will did not know what to say.

'Well?' demanded Rosie. 'Do you think that if I

found myself beginning to like someone, that I should lay aside all my talents and hopes and wishes in order to follow him, even if I ended up frozen and homeless? Do you think that?'

Will wondered vaguely how he'd got into the middle of this, tripped over something that didn't actually seem to be there, and had a weak go at clearing his throat.

'I do not understand it properly,' he said, 'but it sounds as if it would be a terrible waste. Why, you have gifts and brains enough for two, you do.'

Rosie gave him a sharp glance, and Will knew he must have said something more than commonly stupid.

But Rosie repeated his words thoughtfully as she walked along.

'Brains enough for two,' she said.

And now I begin to find myself.

Once I had learning, I feel sure; it is all misty, hidden, now, but then that is safer.

Purple for the King—but I am master, yes, yes. And shall be, yes, again, before too long.

My sister did it. What, I do not yet know. But I shall have the upper hand of her once more. The whip hand.

Red and blue and green.

I must think which way to turn the world. What colour is revenge?

115

Chapter 19

'Not more than another half hour's walk, Mrs Keen,' said Mr Gilfry. 'And then we should be seeing the Red House.'

Mrs Keen stopped for a moment to heave at her large bosom, and to put her hand to the stitch in her side. 'This is the furthest I've come since I was a girl,' she said. 'And what a holiday *this* has turned out to be, Mr Gilfry.'

'And there is still no sign of the captain,' said Miss Winter, who had walked most of the last five miles backwards. 'He must have been caught up in some other affair. Or perhaps we shall find him waiting for us.'

'Such a *very* fine gentleman, to be sure,' said Mrs Keen, tactfully. 'But who can tell what has happened, there, ma'am. I'm afraid a handsome face is but little protection against the trials of war.'

The wind had turned as Will had foretold, bringing in ochrous clouds, and the air felt softer on their faces. They were travelling a little downhill, now, through sad unploughed fields and hedgerows studded with the scarlets of bittersweet and rose hips. The horses were pulling strongly, so that the walkers had to skip every so often to keep up. The wagon swayed and bounced, for they had come off the main road and here the track was bumpier than ever: with every lurch and dip Will watched for the load to shift or the axles to crack. The sheets of grey ice in the ruts were beginning to ooze water at the edges, and they all had to pick their way carefully, for an unwary footstep might tip the ice and send dirty water shooting freezingly across the bottom of a skirt or up a stockinged leg.

And then it happened. Will had been worrying about it all day, but he'd been wasting his time, for when it came there was not the faintest, tiniest thing he could do about it. The near back wheel rolled onto a sheet of ice and then down through it, crushing it to sugar, going in deep, deeper, while the other three wheels rolled along high and dry. The overloaded joints of the wagon moaned and strained.

And then there was a *crack!* even louder than the other noises, and an awful splintering.

The horses, pulled to a vicious halt, threw back their heads in whinnying alarm.

'Whoa! Whoa, there! Good lads!'

Will found himself stone-struck with horror and dismay.

There were voices calling all round him.

'I knew it! I knew it would give way. Well, we're done for, now, and that's for sure.'

The wagon was all a tangle, a disaster.

Will took a deep breath to steady himself.

'What has happened? It is not my brother? Has he fallen?'

'Oh my poor heart,' said Mrs Keen. 'Whatever else can befall us?'

'Will!' called Mr Gilfry, sharply. 'Will, what's amiss? Will?'

Will's knees more or less gave way. He peered through the spokes of a wheel.

'He's looking, Mr Gilfry!'

That was Sam's voice, shrill with excitement.

Something deep red was bulging down from the floor of the wagon nearly to the ground. For a moment, wildly, Will thought the wagon was wounded: but no, of course it was only the rug from the drawing room. Will and Toby had lugged it down the stairs only yesterday, straining and huffing and sneezing as they went.

Will looked again. Some of the floor planks of the wagon had given way. That was what had happened. Look, there was the sharp semi-circle of a broken knot hole. That spot would have been weak even without the streaks of rot that had blistered the old paintwork. And when that plank had given way, two or three of its neighbours had snapped, too, and dug into the road to brake the wagon.

Mr Gilfry listened to Will's report, and nodded, grimly.

'Well, it could be worse,' he said.

'Can it be mended?' asked Miss Winter. 'Shall we be able to continue?'

Mr Gilfry rubbed his chin.

'I think something might be contrived, ma'am. But it'll take time.'

Miss Winter looked up at the white sun that was descending into the lemon clouds.

'But how much time? A stop might give the captain time to find us, but it is beginning to get dark.'

'That depends what we find when the wagon's unloaded, ma'am. If it's only a few planks that've gone, then we can most probably make do with filling in the gap with branches. But they'll have to be cut and sawn.'

'But it will be full dark in an hour.'

'Yes, ma'am. And I'm afraid this will take longer than that.'

Miss Winter had lost her earlier glow. Her pale face looked round the circle grouped uncertainly behind the wagon.

'Then what is to be done? What can be done? We cannot stay out all night. The draughts will be dangerous for us all, and especially for my brother.'

The master had remained quiet during the afternoon, but he had begun to shiver distressingly. He was so slumped in his seat that it was only his bonds that kept him from sliding down onto the road.

Toby rolled his eyes at the great billowing clouds, worn ragged underneath, that were steaming in across the sky.

'I reckon it'll be drenching down, soon, too,' he observed, and walked away muttering something about agues and chills and frostbite.

But here was Sam popping up, bright and excited and full of importance.

'I think there's a house just a little way ahead,' he said. 'There's trails of smoke going up. I saw them. Must be quite a big place.'

Will took in a quick breath of hope with the damp air.

'If they would take in the master, and the mistress, perhaps—'

'Never mind that,' said Rosie. 'As long as they've got a stable that'll give us shelter for the night. It's getting up to a nasty damp cold; and Toby's right, that wind's bringing in a downpour.'

Miss Winter was frowning.

'A house?' she echoed. 'You must be mistaken, Samuel.'

Sam gave her one resentful look and hung his head.

'Well, speak up!' said Rosie. 'Up and tell the mistress what you saw, Sam!'

'Only smoke, ma'am,' mumbled Sam.

'But smoke from where?' asked Miss Winter. 'You would not be able to see the smoke from the Red House from here.'

'A new-built house, maybe, ma'am,' suggested Mrs Keen. 'You said yourself you have not been here for many years. But still, whoever they are, surely they would not turn poor stranded strangers away into such a night as this looks to be.'

There was no point in beginning the unloading of the wagon. They man-handled first Mr Gilfry and then the master down from the body of the wagon. The master came down easily, as limp as an old corpse, but as soon as his feet touched the ground he came disconcertingly to life, and he'd scuttled under the wagon like a large black spider before anyone could think of stopping him. He squatted there, crouching and rocking and twitching away from every peering figure.

Toby scratched his head.

'We could take him along slung across one of the horses' backs,' he said. 'Well, we could if we could get him out.'

But the master shrank away when they tried to grab him, and Miss Winter's nervous stammerings could not move him one inch.

'He has such strength of mind,' she said, bending down to peer at the dark shape that clutched the kaleidoscope. 'Arthur. Arthur, it is all right. We are going to find shelter.'

But at that he waddled backwards even further, so that his skinny back was pressed against the inside of a wheel.

Sister. That's her.

What does she want? I am all in pieces.

Keep away. Keep away, for I am not strong enough to fight you yet.

'Perhaps if we left him behind, he would follow,' suggested Toby. 'There's no point in us all getting wet through and chilled to the bone.'

Rosie came up close behind Will.

'You try, Will,' she suggested. 'You've been with the master as much of any of us. He might trust you.'

'Me?' asked Will, amazed that she thought he might be able to do anything.

'Two fools together,' she said. 'Might make the poor man feel at home. No harm in trying, anyway, is there?'

So Will tried.

'There,' he said, awkwardly, with his great knobbly knees thawing the frozen road to ooze and his heart filled with scared pity. 'It's only me, master. It's only Will. No one couldn't ever be afraid of Will.'

I have known this one.
He is nobody and nothing.
And if I am with him, the rest cannot come so close.

Will moved a little, slowly, not directly towards the master, but to the side, as he might approach a strange dog.

'There,' said Will, again. 'That's better. We must find you somewhere where there is light, sir, so you'll be able to look in your kaleidoscope, and then everything will be back in its pattern and you shall be safe again. You can travel on one of the horses, and you shall soon be there, all comfortable and peaceful. It will give your mind time to settle after all this disturbance. Here, you shall hold onto the kaleidoscope, sir, and we shall go together, the master, and Will from home, two by two. That's it. Steady, now. Keep by me, and I shall keep the world away. That's it.'

The master's jerking fits seemed more or less to have subsided, so they lifted him onto one of the horses. Will and Toby walked close beside him to steady him, and Sam led the other horse. Mrs Keen came last, pushing Mr Gilfry in the bath chair.

'And this is the Red House, after all,' said Miss Winter, as they turned between two pillars on either side of a driveway. 'Though I can never remember seeing smoke from the road before. But then, I have only been here in high summer, I suppose. That must be why. I remember how glad I always was to see those stone gryphons, for it meant we were on holiday. That was before my father died, of course. My brother set his mind against the disturbance of removing here from the first. What a good thing the fires are lit, so we will be able to give any visitors a proper welcome.'

They turned the sweep of the drive as dark was beginning to settle. They had long been smelling rain, and clouds were streaming over like great black cushions of smoke. Chilly breezes were scooping up coats and skirts and trying to tug them away.

'There are the chimneys,' said Mr Gilfry, pointing past the heavy tree tops that stirred and swayed and circled.

'I hope they have plenty of victuals in,' said Mrs Keen, 'for I'm hungry enough to eat a horse, with its saddle for pudding.'

Everyone walked faster.

'*Behind the trees, behind the trees,*' sang the squeaky wheels of the bath chair.

Now I remember. Yes. This is the place. This is the place where they brought me. It dazzled me, deafened me.

I heard their laughter during the terrible days.

My sister was small, hardly more than a kitten. And then the stranger came who gave me poison. They called him doctor, but he made holes in my skin, made holes in my mind, and however much I screamed he had no pity.

I tasted the poison again, this morning.

My sister brought it.

But behind the trees was ruin.

Chapter 20

Even the cellars of the Red House were roofless and vandalized: the bottle-racks had been pushed over and smashed. A barrel, in girth nearly as big as one of the cartwheels, had been hacked through with a blade.

'I bet that was a good drop of beer, that was, too,' said Toby, regretfully, shaking his fat cheeks over the damage.

Will winced away from the hack-marks in the side of the oak barrel. It would have been a fine sharp blade to do such damage, and wielded by a strong and skilful arm: an arm skilled in destruction. He shuddered at the thought.

The main door to the house leaned half off its hinges. Will lifted it straight and stepped inside. Everything he could see was black and burned beyond hope. He put a cautious amount of weight on the bottom tread of the stairs, but the wood, black in a sooty cross-hatch of charcoal, cracked under his foot.

'There's no point in going up there,' said Toby, behind him. 'Look here, there's nowhere to get to.'

A doorway led into what was now almost a tower. Will looked up and up, past fireplaces that clung incongruously to the walls, to parallels of still-smoking beams that had once held up a roof.

A tiled roof, it must have been: the floor was ankle-deep in jagged shards of terracotta. Will went to take a step further in, but Toby caught his arm.

'Don't you go in there,' he said. 'Those beams will more than likely come down and crack your head open like an egg.'

Solid oak, those beams would have been, cut from a tree that might have been an acorn five hundred years ago. A century a-growing, and hundreds of years of sturdy work, destroyed in a few hours.

Outside the voices of Mrs Keen and Rosie were railing in high anger and bewildered indignation. Will and Toby exchanged glances: it would be easiest to leave the women to simmer down a bit.

'We'd best walk round the house,' suggested Toby. 'See if there is anywhere where we might shelter for the night.'

The house had been built of ghostly cream stone that loomed through the dimness. In one room Will saw, high up, some painted birds chasing across some wallpaper, the precious work of distant, ancient artists. Will gazed up at it. Perhaps that bird there could be saved, for some fortunate draught had left it hardly burned at all. He might be able ever-so-gently to peel away the picture from the wall. It was a fine bird with a gilded beak, and it was worth saving.

'Oh yes, good idea,' said Toby, when Will suggested it. 'Put it on the list of things to do, Will. At about number six hundred and fifty-six.'

The house had been torched in several places. Toby picked up a bottle in one room, then swore and dropped it again very swiftly.

'Brandy,' he said, shaking the burn from his hand. 'They must have poured spirits over everything to make it burn properly.' He looked round sadly. 'They've made a good job of it, I'll give them that.'

Will sighed, and shook his head.

'There's no good here,' he said. 'Look at this!'

He prodded a partly charred board with his boot.

'What is it?'

'Walnut. Say three men's lives in the growing, and who can say how much skill in the fashioning. Look, you can just see, it has been cut across a burr. You would have been able to see pictures in it—pictures that'd been locked up for a hundred years—and if you'd cut it in a different place there'd have been another picture, just as wonderful. But now . . . ' He took a deep breath. 'This sickens me.'

'I wonder where their dung-heap is. They couldn't have harmed that, could they?'

'But why should *anything* have been harmed?'

Toby shrugged.

'It's the war. That's what it's about, harming things.'

Will thought about the captain, bright and shining and fine. And about George, so brave and clever.

'I don't understand,' he said. And he comforted himself that there must be a good reason for all this, if only he were clever enough to work it out.

* * *

Miss Winter was sitting on the deserted front steps of the house, exhausted, and on the verge of tears. The master was crouched in a stony corner near her, rocking and muttering and banging the kaleidoscope over and over again on one bony thigh. Will went across to the gazebo where he had parked Mr Gilfry: but Mr Gilfry was asleep and snoring in his chair. Will left him, glad to find someone at peace.

He was wondering how many of them might be able to sleep in a circular gazebo with a stone floor and only the most ornamental of roofs, when someone called him.

'Will!'

And here was Sam, racing along as fast as he could.

'There's a barn!' Sam called. 'I've found a big barn behind the trees. And there's hay in it, and all!'

He arrived in a scatter of gravel and a flurry of joyful expectation, like a welcoming spaniel.

Will smiled at him.

'Good lad,' he said. 'You'd better show me where it is, then.'

It was strange how life went on so nearly as usual in its pattern. Sam and Toby headed out into the skirling blue dusk of the woods to find fuel for a fire, Will contrived a tripod that would suspend a pot over it, Mrs Keen cooked supper, and Rosie fashioned the hay into beds. In some ways things were as they had always been.

It was harder on those who had lost their places altogether. The mistress was mistress of nowhere— and the master was master not even of himself. He sat and rocked and hummed to himself.

'He was sometimes so as a boy,' said Miss Winter, wearily. 'He is many years my senior, of course, but I do remember. It would often take me hours to coax him back to us, but I had the patience of the very young, then. The doctors declared that he would never speak any more; and then they gave no hope of his ever reading; but I think I was too small to be a threat to him, and once he decided to listen to me, he mastered his alphabet all in an afternoon.'

'The master was lucky to have such a sister to care for him,' said Mrs Keen.

'But where is the captain?' said Miss Winter, shivering.

Mrs Keen had supper ready by the time Will, damp and thoroughly chilled, had finished going backwards and forwards through the blustery wind and brought back from the wagon the last load of things they needed for the night.

'I suppose it is too late for anyone to be travelling, now,' said Miss Winter, bleakly.

'I'm glad we thought to bring a lantern,' said Mr Gilfry.

'And thank providence I thought to bring this ham,' said Mrs Keen. 'Though how we are to cut it to be sure I do not know, for my carving knife is buried deep on the wagon.'

'Will,' said Mr Gilfry. 'You have your knife with you.'

Will's old knife was second-hand, and concave with use, but it was a great treasure for all that, and Mr Gilfry had taught him to keep it as sharp as a January frost.

'Give it here, then,' said Mrs Keen, busily, stirring the pot of oats with one hand.

Will hesitated.

'Let Will carve,' said Mr Gilfry. 'It's his knife, after all.'

Carving was not difficult, though it was surprising, at first, the way the meat eased itself away from the blade.

'You're not making a bad job of that,' admitted Mrs Keen, a little surprised.

Toby gave a snort.

'But what have we come to, that Will should carve, eh? That he should be master of the company!'

Will paused, astonished. He was only a foundling (a *dumpling*, Rosie had once said), and yet . . .

He laid his knife against the gleaming orange rind of the ham once more.

My mind is settling.

Yes, but onto islands in a drifting sea.

And there is my sister. I see her, I see her. I do not know, though, if she can see me.

There are others, too: traitors, poisoners, murderers?

I have forgotten how to tell.

Gentlefolk had book-learning and knowledge, but sometimes learning could not help them. The master would not even look at his food, and when Miss Winter put it to his lips he batted the spoon away and sprayed Toby with bits of pudding.

'Will,' said Mr Gilfry. 'You try, boy.'

Will tried, but the master hissed and turned his face towards the wall. Will gave up quite soon, out of pity, and instead built up a wall of hay around the man and left him in peace.

'Look, Will has made a pattern on the plate with pieces of ham,' said Sam, doubtfully. 'Mrs Keen will scold him for playing with the food.'

'Will hoped it would comfort the master,' said Rosie, swiftly.

They put the dishes outside in the blustery rain. 'I can hardly bear to leave them dirty overnight,' said Mrs Keen, her forehead wrinkled into worm-like hummocks of orange in the light of the lantern, 'for I never have held with such slatternly ways. But there, it's so blamed dark I could no more find water to wash the dishes than a pot of gold!'

Miss Winter sighed.

'I suppose it can't be helped,' she said. 'And I suppose my brother will know nothing of it. But what if someone arrives, and sees them?'

'No one will be out a-riding on a night like this, ma'am,' said Mrs Keen.

They had pulled down hay to make beds for the men.

'And where will you sleep?' asked Mr Gilfry,

catching Sam, whose excitement meant that he could hardly bear to be still. 'With your sister, or with the men?'

'With the men,' he declared, with great dignity and indignation.

'Now you keep well away while I go up the ladder, Sam,' said Mrs Keen. 'For if I fall down on top of you I'll squash you as flat as a pancake, to be sure.'

'Sam!' came Rosie's voice from near the roof. 'You settle down, now, and go to sleep. Because if you cause any disturbance you'll have me to answer to.'

'And me,' said Mr Gilfry, drily.

The scuffling over in the corner stopped abruptly, and Will found himself grinning to himself. Now that people had stopped moving about, the darkness of the storm outside seemed to have grown thicker, like churning velvet.

'Put out the lantern, Will,' said Mr Gilfry. 'And close the door against the wind. There's a proper gale brewing out there, for sure.'

'Watch out everybody, now,' said Will. 'It's so black I might tread on you.'

'How can we watch out when it's as thick as a rat-hole at midnight?' demanded Toby. 'Just keep away from me with your great—ow! Ow!'

'Sorry,' said Will, humbly, falling over. He landed on a heap of hay, and hoped it was his bed. He groped for his jacket and pulled it over him, burrowing his feet into the hay for warmth.

He lowered his head carefully against the prickling stems and let the scent of it comfort him.

They slept, that night, all of them, exhausted and dirty and footsore and homeless as they were. The hay held the warmth of their bodies, and in the stillness of the barn their soft breath hovered over them like a coverlet.

Will woke once and opened his eyes to the darkness. The wind had died down, and around him there were people breathing. Rosie was up in the loft, only a few feet away. He imagined her, curled under her coat: not standing straight and sharp and ready as she usually was, but relaxed and warm and contented. And soft. So soft . . .

He wished the night could go on for ever.

There were too many dead.

One would have been too many, of course, but eight of our company were corpses, and there were others we could not find. We made shelters against the rain with our muskets and blankets, and squatted together in the mud all night. Oh, we shall joke about it one day.

An officer came by.

'Who is in charge here?' he asked. And we did not know, for our sergeant was dead, and our corporal missing. So I upped and told the officer (for the others were not so used to talking

to quality, they mostly having been labourers).
And the officer said, well, you *seem a likely lad*;
and made me corporal.

And I felt proud and strong enough to
take on all the enemy.

Chapter 21

In the clear inevitable daylight the ruins of the house were heart-breaking. Last night, in the dimness, it had been bad enough, but it had at least had a mystery and even beauty about it: but now the destruction was laid open—plain, and throat-catching, and ugly as sin.

Will walked round the house twice, hoping to find something that had escaped the flames. The only sign of what must have been the kitchen was a huge pot-hook and a row of copper discs in decreasing sizes—a whole set of pans, probably. Heaps of ash, somehow sheltered from the rain, rose around him and made him sneeze.

And here was a trail of small footsteps denting a path through the cinders. Will looked up and just caught a glimpse of a coat-tail whisking out of sight through a doorway.

'Sam!' he called.

There was a pause, and then an untidy fair head came slowly back into sight.

'Come here,' said Will. 'No, not through the building! Come round by the path.'

Sam slid round the corner and halted carefully out of arm's reach.

'Don't you know one of those oak roof beams might come down and kill you?' asked Will; although Sam must have known, because Will had explained it to him at least twice.

Sam took a step backwards, but Will was quicker. He reached out a long arm and put a hand on Sam's shoulder. 'Now you listen to me,' said Will. 'We can't manage without you, Sam. We need you to see to the horses.'

Sam considered a little.

'Will you tell Rosie I was in the house?' he asked.

'You just keep yourself safe, Sam, or else she'll only have bits of your bones to scold.'

Rosie had found a horse trough to wash the dishes in. Her hands were bright, bright pink with cold, and Will wanted to hold them against his skin and let his warmth comfort them. He dried the dishes for her and carried them back to the barn.

'Everything has gone wrong, Will,' said Rosie, holding up her skirts to save them from the drenching grey dew. 'The wagon has broken down, and the master is ill; and now we have found this house destroyed. Where shall we go? And what shall we find when we get there? That captain yesterday, he was a fine strong man, but plainly he has greater things to do than look after us, whatever the poor mistress is hoping for. Is there nothing we can do to keep ourselves safe?'

'I don't know, Rosie,' said Will, shaking his head. 'I can't say which way the world will turn.

But . . . well, I know it's not much help, but I can only promise that, whatever happens, I shall be there, too.'

Rosie opened her mouth: but then found nothing to say.

'I take it we shall not be staying here, Miss Winter, after all,' said Mr Gilfry. The dawn had brought colour back to the world, but his face was still grey with the exhaustion of pain.

Miss Winter hesitated, and sighed.

'I do not see how it is possible,' she said. 'Even if we could rebuild enough of the house to live in, this place is dangerous. But then to be travelling is dangerous, too. Oh, how I wish the captain had been able to join us. He would have been able to decide all this.'

Mr Gilfry nodded understandingly.

'Indeed, ma'am. Well, if we cannot stay, then we must move on. Move south, away from the rebels.'

She shook her head, but only helplessly.

'I suppose so. Maybe we will catch up with the captain again, and then he can advise us where to find refuge. If there *is* any refuge: it is hard to believe we are anything more than leaves in a storm. I suppose we must make for the town. There will be inns there.'

Mr Gilfry hesitated.

'There will be many folk there ahead of us,' he said. 'And the town will be a magnet for the troops.'

'Yes, I know,' said Miss Winter, wearily. 'But I can think of nothing better we can do.'

It took over an hour to unload the back part of the great blue wagon. Miss Winter wandered up and down between the barn, where her brother rocked and scowled and turned his kaleidoscope, and the road. The gale was nearly spent, leaving great drifts of lemon maple leaves tumbled in the wheel ruts.

On the wagon there were four planks broken; luckily they had snapped cleanly, without doing any damage to the axle.

'Which is near half a miracle,' said Mr Gilfry, supervising the work from his chair.

'Not that we've got anything to patch the hole with,' said Toby, mournfully.

'We spoke of branches, before,' Rosie reminded them.

'Well, we certainly don't lack for those,' said Mr Gilfry, looking round.

'No, Mr Gilfry,' agreed Will. 'But the barn door might be better. That's got some stout timber in it.'

Mr Gilfry tipped back his head and gave Will a considering look.

'All right,' he said at last. 'Off you go. You've got your claw hammer, Will?'

'Yes, Mr Gilfry.'

'And take Toby, too, to help carry the thing.'

They got the door off its hinges with no more than the usual difficulty. It was a solid piece of timber, sure enough.

'Stop, stop,' puffed Toby, after a hundred yards of carrying it. 'You're going too fast. Let me rest a minute.'

Will put the door down and took the opportunity to stretch his fingers.

And then he noticed something shiny on the ground.

He picked it up. It was a button, that was all. A brass button, such as a soldier might wear. It was stamped with a fine king's crown. A button from a king's man, then.

Will gazed at it, very puzzled, the skeleton of the Red House rising starkly behind him.

The wagon was ready to travel by mid-morning, but by then the workers were in need of a rest. And then there were still the horses to harness, and the master to coax back onto his place on the wagon.

'I hope the master is more himself today,' said Mr Gilfry. 'He's not easy to manage.'

'He is quieter, certainly,' said Miss Winter. 'He has not been lashing out so much, except when I tried to wipe his face. And then I think he imagined I had designs on the kaleidoscope.'

'Will is the one to look after him,' said Rosie. 'The master knows he can trust him.'

'All ready, Will?' asked Mr Gilfry, a little while later.

'Just checking the linchpins, Mr Gilfry. You never

know but that someone might have been up to mischief.'

'That's a thought. A good thought, lad. You know, I could not have managed without you, just lately.'

Will smiled up at Mr Gilfry and found him suddenly old. Old, and grey. Will's heart bumped with alarm.

'You'll soon be mended, Mr Gilfry,' he said. 'And as strong as ever, I'll warrant.'

Mr Gilfry's mouth smiled a little, but there was doubt lurking in his eyes.

'I do not see any sign of it, Will, to tell the truth. My leg seems—it seems more painful than ever.'

Will's heart bumped again. It must be bad for Mr Gilfry to admit so much.

'I'll find a cushion for your leg, Mr Gilfry,' he said hastily. 'That must help a little. It'll not take a minute.'

It was a fine embroidered cushion, probably a month's work from Miss Winter's thin fingers.

'Just there, lad. That's it. That's it. Yes, that's easier, I thank you.'

'Let's find another for your ankle.'

'Thank you. Thank you,' said Mr Gilfry, again, when Will had him settled as well as he could. 'You know, Will, that if . . . that if George . . . ' Mr Gilfry had to stop to clear his throat. 'George himself could not have taken better care of me than you have done.'

George: Rosie's sweetheart.

Will forced himself to speak cheerfully.

'George will be with us again soon, Mr Gilfry. In *thirteen moons*, he said—but with all this fighting I expect he is busy. He won't be long finding us, though, we may be sure.'

Mr Gilfry shook his head.

'I do not believe that George will come back,' he said, quietly. 'We have not heard from him, and all the others have managed to get messages home. I feel it in my heart that he is dead, Will.'

Mr Gilfry was a sensible man, a man to see things plainly; and Will found himself bewildered by a mixture of appalled loss and a horrible stringy hope.

'It is a bitter thing to have no means of making my own living, and to have no son, either, to support my old age,' said Mr Gilfry. 'And to know I must in the end be a burden upon the parish.'

Will frowned. Mr Gilfry, going on the parish? There had been cripples in the almshouse, for sure: people without families, or whose families were themselves too poor to support them. Small and white, they had seemed, even to Will as a little boy. It was worse to be a cripple than a child, for at least the children could work and earn part of their living. The cripples merely lingered greyly, ghosts even while their hearts continued to beat.

Will had long known it was a very uncertain thing to be dependent on the kindness of others.

'You need not go on the parish while I am here,' he said, stoutly. 'You are wise, and I am strong, now, so we shall manage well enough.'

Mr Gilfry smiled, but shook his head.

'That is a promise you had best not make, Will. I would not wish to think that more lives than mine were wasted by a foolish accident.'

'It wouldn't be wasted,' said Will, without it ever occurring to him that he was answering back. 'I shall look after you until you are better, or until George comes. I give you my word of it.'

The master was quiet enough: more settled than his usual self, even. Will helped him up onto his seat, talking softly all the while, and tied him there securely, but leaving his hands free.

'Will,' said Mr Gilfry, quietly, as he finished. 'I'm saying this to you now, because I do not know what the world shall bring us today, nor if tomorrow will ever come. But I have never been certain that George is truly my son. I was a soldier, you see, and we had won a victory . . . and then George's mother turned up, later, with a babe for me to care for. But I would be surprised if she had not known other men, too wise to give their names. But, Will, even knowing that, I found I could not watch a boy grow up and not feel about him as a father does.'

Will, confused and embarrassed, climbed hastily back down to the ground and did not even try to think about what Mr Gilfry was telling him.

'I cannot help but fear for the safety of the captain,' said Miss Winter, staring back along the road. 'Surely he would have taken leave of us, if he could have done so.'

The road curled back through the weeping trees, endless, and quite empty.

My mind has come together and now I can order the world again.

Red, blue, green . . .

Every pattern is possible. I must turn and watch the tumbling colours until everything falls into place.

And then I will be able to get rid of the traitors. All of them.

They were all stiff from unaccustomed exercise and strange beds. Even Mrs Keen could not but be a little cast down.

'Waking up on a bed of hay has brought it home to me that I have *lost* my home,' she said. 'And my kitchen, too. It is silly to mourn for pans, but, there, it catches my heart to know I am walking away from them, and from all the happy times I've had with them in my hands.'

'I know what it's like,' said Toby. 'Five years I've been tending my dunghill. It's a bereavement, that's what it is.'

Rosie rolled her eyes.

'That's hardly the same,' she said. 'It's not like being wrenched away from someone you've depended on, as I have with George. It's not like knowing that perhaps I'll never see him again.'

'But we must all keep on hoping,' said Miss Winter, urgently. 'Otherwise there is no point in carrying on.'

Mrs Keen sighed.

'Aye, ma'am,' she said. 'We must hope that all the chances of war fall our way. You know, I keep myself cheerful by remembering the first time I saw

143

Mr Keen. He was a footman, then, and he was carrying a chamber pot, as I recall, but it was as if a dam had burst inside my heart. All the pent-up love of a lifetime, erupting inside me. Ah yes,' she went on, wistfully. 'I was only fourteen years old; but that makes the feelings all the stronger, for happening in an emptier skull.'

'Yes,' said Miss Winter, with a sigh. 'And perhaps being swept away is better than dying of thirst.'

Rosie frowned.

'But some people, even young ones, can be sensible in their choices, all the same,' she said. 'There are more important things than fancies and eruptions, after all, for all the bursting dams.'

'Certainly there are,' said Mrs Keen. 'But there, love comes along with his sharp arrows, and ten to one he makes fools of us, all the same.'

Will thought about arrows. He imagined himself with a bow in his hands, with the string cutting into his finger, and the strength of the yew pulling against his arm. He imagined a boy (almost a man, he was) standing beyond the delicate tip of the arrow.

And suddenly Will wanted Rosie so much he almost groaned. He wanted to hold her tightly, tightly, with every part of himself: to hold her until they were part of each other for ever.

And then he wanted to rest his head on her and sleep.

Chapter 22

They halted after a while to allow the horses to stale. Sam went off into the trees and came back clutching a switch that whizzed through the air very satisfyingly.

'I do not know where he gets the energy for such foolishness,' said Rosie, half weary, half exasperated, as Sam, tripping slightly over an ant-hill, came close to taking Toby's nose off. 'Sam! Put that down, or I'll be after you!'

Will offered the master a drink, and this time the man sipped quietly at the cup Will held for him.

'I will soon destroy them,' the master said, with satisfaction, raising thin wet lips.

It was such a shock to hear him speak that Will nearly fell backwards off the wagon.

'Will—will you, sir?'

The master hunched his head further into his bony shoulders.

'Oh yes. I did not realize, but I see it, now. The tower limited me. I needed to take a larger view.' He threw a fierce glance into Will's eyes for just an instant. 'And it will soon be done.'

Will, very shaken, went to find Rosie.

'The master spoke to me,' he told her.

'What did he say?'

Will thought about it.

'I am not sure,' he admitted at last. 'He might have been talking about the war, perhaps.'

Rosie gave an exasperated sigh as she hoisted her pack again.

'That's typical of a man, that is: either crazy, unconscious, or fighting. Sometimes I think fighting's all you men ever really care about.'

'Well,' said Will, seriously, 'it's something that must be cared about. We can hardly ignore it, after all, can we?'

'But what good is it?' Rosie asked, exasperated. 'All it does is make widows and orphans and ruins and broken promises, that's all.'

'I think it must do a bit more than that,' said Will, mildly.

'Oh, you would say that. I suppose it gives grown men the chance to dress in bright coats and varnished boots, and to ride fast, and take what and whom you please. You know, I could quite fancy the life myself.'

'It . . . it decides things,' said Will. 'That's what war does.'

Rosie snorted.

'I suppose it decides which shade of fancy coat is worn in which piece of the country.'

'Yes. And it decides matters of . . . of policy, Rosie. And justice. I know they are things that I do not understand,' he went on, hurriedly, 'but there are those with more brains and knowledge than me—'

'You amaze me,' said Rosie.

'—and they direct what should be done. To obey a great man—like the captain, yesterday—would be something, Rosie, that I—that, if things had been different, I should have felt myself honoured to do.'

Rosie laughed for quite a long time, and Will felt himself flush to the roots of his hair.

'I know I am not fit to take part in it,' he said, 'and I did not say I was. I only said—'

'I know. I know, Will, you fool. But listen. Do you think it is all like a game of chess? With a black side and a white side, all drawn up?'

'Well—'

'In a game of chess, which side fights for good, and which for evil?'

'Well—'

'And if it were decided amongst the players that the loser would forfeit his life, would the pawns on his side play harder for him?'

Rosie was so sharp she could dance circles round Will's poor brain. He was still blinking and frowning when she answered her own question.

'No, they won't, because the pawn has a head of solid ivory and does not understand the politics or the policy or the right and wrong. And that is what a soldier is, Will: a pawn in a game where he is never told the rules or purpose. That is why he has to be given a bright coat and a musket, and a trumpet to announce him; to let him pretend he has importance, so he will cast away his life and think it a reasonable bargain.'

Will bowed his head.

'You're clever, Rosie,' he said. 'I know I cannot think like you can, and work out the rights of it all. So I suppose it's lucky that I am not a soldier, for it's true, I would not even know which side to fight for. So it's a good thing that I have given my word to Mr Gilfry that I will never leave him, not for anything, while he has need of me.'

Rosie turned to him, and suddenly her eyes were shining.

'Have you, Will? Truly? Have you given your word?'

Will gaped—and found himself so utterly, dizzily confused and adrift that he wasn't even all that sure which way up he was. He needed so desperately to get hold of Rosie, to touch her perfect skin, that he had to put his hands behind his back and hold them there in case he should accidentally do it.

'There is no one else to look after Mr Gilfry while George is gone,' he said, at last, waveringly, feeling as if he were swallowing a great pebble with the word *George*. 'And Mr Gilfry, he has been good to me, for all my foolishness. So I thought . . . I thought I should, somehow, Rosie.'

Rosie was still looking at him and he had a sudden conviction that he was never going to feel his feet on solid ground again.

'Yes,' she said, and she seemed a little puzzled,

too. 'George is gone. And if—when—he comes back, then—'

'—then Mr Gilfry will have a son again, and he won't need me any more,' said Will, earnestly. 'I know that. I know I can't take George's place, Rosie, even if . . . even if . . . '

But Rosie's lips were plump and parted, and Will was now so muddled that he couldn't find his way to the end of that sentence: his brain was tumbling over itself so dizzily that he'd even forgotten how to walk.

Rosie took a step towards him, until the gathers over her bosoms were only half a foot away from his chest. He froze, mesmerized, for a long, fascinating, appalling, somersaulting moment.

'There are others, besides Mr Gilfry, that need looking after now George is gone,' she said.

Will, peering terrified through the curls of steam that were emanating from his every pore, cast around wildly for her meaning. She could not mean—no. Surely not.

'I have done my best, Rosie,' he stammered. 'I am not George, of course, I know that, but I have taken his place as best I can.'

She was looking at him as if she were waiting for something; he could feel her gaze on him, though he did not dare look at her face, or anywhere else, because somehow he found he'd squeezed his eyes tight shut.

'You are a great, great fool, Will Nunn,' said Rosie, at last, with a sigh of huge regret. And something soft and warm brushed against his cheek.

When he finally got up courage to open his eyes, he was alone and left behind on the cold muddy road.

We celebrated our victory quietly, grimly, with a wry toast to the fallen (fallen, ripped in two, impaled on gleaming steel, and left to flail in agony to death. Sometimes you can know too much). We dressed our wounds: tended them tenderly, for every drop of blood had been squeezed from all our hearts.

Then orders came, so we packed up, shared our comrades' possessions amongst us, and marched, together, left-right, along the cold road.

I do not say we were eager for battle. Not even for victory.

But we were all of us eager to kill.

Aye.

Chapter 23

They went on for a couple more hours before their next stop. The wagon had still not fallen into any more pieces, and Will knew that his watching and fussing would have no bearing on whether it did or not; but still, he couldn't stop himself doing it.

'There's nothing to be done, unless it does,' said Mr Gilfry, on his high seat. 'We must hope for the best, that's all.'

Will, restless, prowled off to look for Rosie. He felt constantly in need of her, as if he were consumed with thirst—though whenever he found her, saw her, was with her, the thirst did not go away but tormented him all the more. She was up high on the wagon, fumbling at bales and chests, with her skirts getting caught on buckles and her shawl getting snagged on strings.

Will stood and looked up at her—found Toby looking up, too—and had a fleeting and disturbing impulse to punch Toby's heavy face.

'Where's young Sam?' Will demanded, almost at random.

Toby shrugged his round shoulders.

'Not far away, I don't suppose,' he said, squinting

up against the light and hoping, as Will well knew, for a gust of wind to billow Rosie's skirts up.

Will looked around, saw Sam's fair head, and breathed a sigh of relief. Then Will reached up a long arm, and had pulled himself up on to the top of the load without being aware of making any decision to do it.

Rosie, flushed from stooping, gave him only a glance.

'Miss Winter needs new shoes,' she said. 'The ones she's wearing are worn right through: they weren't made for walking all these miles over these rough roads. I know we have any number of pairs in here somewhere, but all I can find is a pair of slippers.'

Will scratched his head.

'I could cut her some sacking to wrap round her feet,' he suggested.

'Oh, don't be so foolish!' snapped Rosie. 'Miss Winter isn't a beggar to go around so!'

Will flinched away from her scorn. He had packed this great top-heavy load—half of it twice— so he should know what was in each bundle and chest. Except that he didn't. That box contained Mrs Keen's dishes and spoons, but as for that bundle, or that bale . . . He stood there, balanced on the load, and he hadn't a clue where Miss Winter's shoes might be. If they had to search through every bundle it might take the rest of the day: really, the rest of the day. Will groaned to himself. What should they do? It would be easier to see if Miss

Winter's shoes could be made to do, whatever Rosie—

Will caught sight of a movement back along the road, but by the time he had turned his head to look properly all was still again. What had that been? He'd only caught a glimpse of it. Had it been any more than a woodpecker swooping across the road? No, not a woodpecker: something else that bounced a little, like a woodpecker in flight. Something like—

There was a shout from Sam.

'Horses! Will, I can hear horses!'

Will, up on the load, swept his eyes round the little company: women, boys, madman, cripple.

And Rosie, sweet Rosie, frozen bending forward over an opened sack, with her shawl fallen away from her bosom so that Will could see . . .

'Quick!' said Will. 'Quick, Rosie!' He vaulted down from the load and hit the ground hard, but he was turning round at once and reaching up to Rosie, holding out his hands.

'Quick,' he said again. And she scrambled over towards him, put her hands in his, and slithered down. He was strong enough to guide her down safely. He held her for a glorious split second—but he had to send her away, and quickly, quickly.

Miss Winter was staring along the road, frozen between fear and a struggling hope.

'Perhaps it is the captain,' she said. 'Perhaps—'

'Take Sam and Mrs Keen and Miss Winter,' said Will to Rosie. 'Get them out of sight in the trees. Quick.'

He looked round again. Mr Gilfry could not move, but the black twig-bundle beside him could shift itself, if it would.

'You must take cover, sir,' said Mr Gilfry to the master. 'Will will show you the way. He will show you somewhere to hide.'

But the master only hissed and jerked out spitefully with his elbow when Mr Gilfry tried to reach the knots on his bonds.

Will looked round for Toby. There was no sign of him, but here was Sam running back across the road. Beyond him Rosie was ducking under an iron grey branch, and pulling Miss Winter after her.

The thudding of the horses' hooves was clear, now. Not a large company, but certainly more than one horse.

'Go off and hide yourself, Will,' ordered Mr Gilfry. 'And get Sam away.'

'I'll pull a tarpaulin over us like—'

But even as he said it, it was too late: three gleaming horses had trotted round the corner into plain sight.

'They're King's men,' said Will, seeing their scarlet coats.

'Red,' said the master, in deep satisfaction. 'I wished for some red to go with all this gold. There needs to be blood.'

'King's men, fighting men,' muttered Mr Gilfry. 'How much difference does the colour of their tunics make?'

Will remembered Rosie's chess-piece soldiers,

with their solid heads; and the captain, yesterday, vanishing so neatly over that low wall; and that shining crown-stamped button he'd found in the grounds of the Red House.

'It's three against two, Mr Gilfry,' he said, doubtfully, 'not counting the master.'

'Three against three,' piped up Sam, determined, but pale as a peeled switch.

Mr Gilfry grunted.

'Three armed men against two boys and a cripple,' he said, dourly. 'Now listen to me, lads. If they want anything, they take it. Do you understand me? We've not got anything worth getting killed for.'

They watched the horsemen approach. Mr Gilfry, breathing hard, gave a commentary.

'The one on the black horse is a lieutenant. Yes, and those facings on his jacket are of the Twenty-First: jail-scrapings, the lot of them, when I was a soldier; and I doubt they've improved their manners. The one on the flea-bitten grey's his sergeant, and the fat one's an ensign. A shabby lot altogether. But still, too much for us to take on.'

'We could let off a firecracker, and that might make their horses bolt, Mr Gilfry,' suggested Sam. 'Well, if we had a firecracker we could, anyway.'

Mr Gilfry rolled a perishing eye at him.

'You'd better start holding your tongue and doing as you're bid, young man, or you'll hardly survive what your friends have to settle with you, let alone anyone else.'

The three soldiers rose and fell in their saddles,

taller and stronger than ordinary men. Their uniforms were fine enough for angels, but Rosie's mocking words still echoed in Will's head: *bright coats, and trumpets to announce them*. (Rosie? Where was she? Safe, was all that mattered.)

The lieutenant was a wiry man with a florid face that clashed with his tunic. His eyes were pale and hard. Will ducked his head respectfully towards the silvery mud on the lieutenant's cracked boots.

'Where are you headed?' the lieutenant demanded, just as the captain had done yesterday.

'To town, sir,' answered Mr Gilfry, sturdily. The pale eyes flickered over Sam and focused on Will.

'And what's on the load? Money? Silver? Jewellery?'

The little pieces of glass tumbled in the master's kaleidoscope, round and round. And for a moment Will, dizzily, felt like nothing but a chunk of glass himself, tumbled helplessly as the world turned round him.

'No, sir,' he managed to say. 'The money and silver has been taken separately, sir. I don't know of any jewellery.'

The sergeant began a long low curse, and the lieutenant's lips thinned to a gash.

'Search the wagon,' he barked.

The ensign drew his sabre. The blade shone as bright as the cloudy sky. It was like a sickle, only a thousand times shinier and more dangerous. Will thought of all the carefully packed bales and boxes on the wagon, all fitted together like a piece of marquetry and capable of fitting together in no other way, and he could almost have cursed, himself.

The sergeant urged his horse up to the side of the blue and yellow wagon, secured the reins, kicked his boots free of the stirrups, and climbed up onto the load.

The sergeant had a knife, as well as his sabre. He slit the nearest bale with a back-hand slash that made Will's insides contract with horror. The sergeant bent down with a grunt to tug out a sullen hank of velvet as deep and rich as blood. He grunted again, and moved on to the next bale.

Will saw him drawing back the knife again and he couldn't stand it.

'If you please, sir,' he exclaimed, seizing the wooden side rails to haul himself up. 'If you please, sir, there is no need to cut the bales open. I can open them for you easily enough. Let me help you, sir, if you please.'

He scrambled over the bales and sacks and boxes to where the sergeant stood with his legs well apart to balance himself on the uneven surface.

'Which one would you have me show you, sir?' he said. 'This one? This contains Miss Winter's gowns, I think . . . yes, here, do you see, sir? And this . . . this is a bale of sheets. Fine linen sheets, they are, with a towel or two folded in among them, to help prevent them creasing. And here we have . . . '

The sergeant had already turned away.

'What is this?' he demanded, harshly, indicating a box.

Will hastily balanced his way over.

'I'm not sure of that, sir. Mrs Keen had the packing of that. I could prise off the top for you if you wish. I have my tools here. It would not take a moment.'

'Who is Mrs Keen?' demanded the lieutenant, behind him.

Will turned and ducked his head again, showing respect.

'Mrs Keen is the cook, sir,' he said. 'She was anxious about her cooking pots and spoons, so it's probably some of those. Would you like to see, sir?'

Will wondered at himself, prattling on. It was not like him at all, and neither was the smothering feeling that was pushing up inside him and interfering with his breath. Rosie was in his mind all the time . . . she, and young Sam, whom he rather thought had sensibly ducked down under the wagon out of sight. Between Rosie and Sam it was hard to think clearly about anything else, and he was in terror that he might give them away. Rosie was only a few yards across the road. What might these three do if they knew that?

The ensign had smooth bulging cheeks that were nipped in by his tight collar. The cold air carried thick surges of his perfumed pomade that made Will sick in his stomach.

Will found he was still talking.

'And here, sir, is a little table. A fine table, as you can see, inlaid with mother-of-pearl and rosewood. Very skilled work, and done in the East, far over the sea. We had it in the barn for a while, to put new shellac on, and it took my breath away to see the little patterns, and the strange animals. This creature here, with the long nose that curls round, Mr Gilfry says it is called an elephant. They are very great in size, almost like a house, but they can be tamed and used to carry logs, which they can pick up as easily with their noses as you or I could pick up a single plank.'

'Hold your tongue,' exploded the sergeant, suddenly vicious. Then, turning to the lieutenant, 'I doubt there's anything here of any use to us, sir.'

'I fear not,' said the lieutenant, coldly.

The ensign ran his finger round the inside of his tight collar where it had rubbed his fat neck raw.

'There are the horses, sir.'

The lieutenant rode forward a couple of paces to inspect the great horses that stood patiently blowing clouds of steam and swishing at the winter gnats with their tails.

'They will be a hindrance,' said the lieutenant. 'But then, they are soon sold. All right, ensign. Unhitch the horses, if you please.'

Will looked sharply at Mr Gilfry: but his massive brown back might have been made of stone, for it did not shift an inch.

But if they lost the horses they were stuck, completely stuck, and stranded here for ever.

'They are the only horses we have, sir,' said Will, uncertainly.

The ensign sheathed his sabre, heaved his leg

over his horse's back, and landed with a grunt. He was so plump that his feet looked as small and neat as a lady's.

Will stood, balanced on the uneven top of the wagon and filled with bewilderment. How could this be happening? These were King's men, and Mr Gilfry and Miss Winter and all of them were loyal subjects of the King. They were all honest folk, people who had given up their loved ones for the King's cause.

The ensign had been in the saddle so long that he could hardly walk: he tiptoed and rolled his way to the horses' heads. He ran his small eyes speculatively over the horses' harness, and Will discovered that he hated these soldiers: he loathed them with a hotness and fury as scarlet as their uniforms. He had never hated anybody or anything before, but his ability to feel seemed to have grown, and now this loathing was swelling and growing inside him until he could hardly breathe for it.

But he despised himself almost as much as he did them, for these men were going to strand them, and he was so stupid and useless that he was going to let them do it.

And then, clearly and completely unmistakably, from the black figure that sat, all knees and elbows like some giant spider, came a voice.

'The women are hiding in the trees,' it said. 'Do not neglect to take them, too.'

Chapter 24

There was a long moment when the whole world seemed to have stopped turning—and then everything was accelerating into chaos. The soldiers' heads whipped round towards the thicket of iron-hued ash and burgundy dogwood, and Will, unthinking, threw himself full-length across the wagon and violently into the sergeant's knees. The man folded in the middle, windmilled his arms briefly, lost his hat, and dropped backwards off the high load. There was a hollow *thud*, and then a lesser one, but Will, rushing with fear and exhilaration, was already rolling and pushing himself to his feet.

He glanced around—and froze for a fraction of a second, completely astonished, for up by the horses' heads the ensign's smooth face had gone suddenly mauve. It was like some horrible magic—bright, ugly mauve it was—and the man's eyes were bulging as he clawed with pudgy desperate fingers at his throat.

But there was no time for Will to understand it, for now the pieces in the great kaleidoscope were tumbling all round them and the dizziness of it was threatening to overwhelm him. Now the lieutenant's

horse was rearing up, was screaming in Will's face—
he saw a momentary vision of long yellow teeth and
wide nostrils—and then the iron-clad hooves were
flashing close, close to Will's head, and a horse-
scream of terror was ringing in his ears.

There was a long, awful moment when Will
could not see or think for the shattering sound—and
then everything was spinning on again, randomly,
horrifyingly, impossibly: the lieutenant's florid face,
yes, his whole body and his saddle, too, were sliding
backwards down off his horse. The man clutched at
his reins, and the horse, its head pulled sideways and
backwards, let out another ringing scream and fell,
rolled, and then scrambled up with a huge thumping of hooves and a storm of breath like a smith's
bellows. And then the horse was plunging and running, its saddle abandoned on the ground, and the
lieutenant was left behind it, a scarlet and white
huddle, its sharp elbows up to protect his head.

The wagon suddenly jerked forward and nearly
threw Will off his feet. The carthorses had caught the
infection of terror: they were tossing their heads and
whinnying, pulling against the reins. The sergeant's
grey was trying to tear itself away, too, but it was
tethered and held down.

And now people were running out of the trees.
Will saw them without knowing exactly who they
were. He jumped down to the ground and landed
beside the spread-eagled body of the sergeant. The
man wasn't moving, and at that moment that was
all Will asked for. He snatched up the man's knife

and threw it into the bushes, seized the man's sabre, and ran round to the front of the wagon.

Someone had got hold of the horses' bearing reins, but they were still plunging their heads and stamping their great feet in terror. The ensign was there, on his fat knees. His fingers were dabbing feebly at his purple throat and his eyes were turning upwards.

There was a woman with him. She was hurling his spinning sabre away towards the trees and snatching a gleaming sliver of a knife from his belt. She was bringing it up to his throat.

Will's heart tumbled over itself in horror. He ran forward, but the woman was already tugging the knife across the ensign's swollen neck. Something like a snake fell down by his plump knees. Will gasped in horror—and then dizzily half-realized it was part of the long lash of Mr Gilfry's driving whip.

The ensign gave a long groan, fell forward on his hands, and began to heave in great sobbing breaths, each as rough as a saw's cut.

A face bobbed up in front of Will. Will raised the sabre, but it said 'Will!' and he came to himself and recognized Mrs Keen.

'What . . . ' began Will, rather feebly, through the warm red mist that was surrounding him.

'This one'll be fit for more mischief in a minute,' said Mrs Keen, jerking her head at the ensign. 'We need rope.'

'Will!' called Mr Gilfry, with a sharp edge to his voice. 'Rope! Quick about it!'

Habit found him obeying, climbing back up on to the load. Many of the bales were tied with bits of rope. Will tugged at the knots. One of the sacks came open to expose a bolt of precious oyster-coloured silk to the sky. He climbed down again with lengths of rope flapping from his fist like a handful of eels.

'Him first,' said Mr Gilfry, pointing to where Rosie was standing, a knife in each hand like a pirate, over the ensign. 'Here, you! Over to the fence! Crawl!'

The hotness inside Will was shrivelling rapidly to a horrible chill. He hated this. The ensign was surely no more than a few years older than he was himself, hardly a man, even: George's age. The ensign's huge backside laboured humiliatingly as he crawled. Will suddenly wanted to stop it all: he wanted to take away the knives and sabres and pistols, and even that throttling whip of Mr Gilfry's, and give everybody peace.

'Sit,' said Mr Gilfry, curtly, pointing, as one might to a dog.

The ensign plumped himself down on the drenched grass. He ran a tender finger along the red welt that encircled his neck.

Mrs Keen knew her business.

'Like trussing a goose,' she said. 'And this is the fattest goose I've ever heard tell of, at that.' She forced back the ensign's round shoulders and tugged the rope into neat knots that dragged at the skin of his wrists, securing him to a fence post.

'But surely . . . should we go off and leave him here?' Will ventured, uneasily.

Mrs Keen brushed the mud off her hands.

'I expect someone will come along sooner or later, Will.'

'Sam!' said Rosie's voice, sharply; and Will jumped, and turned.

Sam's eyes and mouth were round with awe and shock and wonder.

'Get the ensign a drink, if you please, Sam,' said Rosie. 'And then go and find Toby and tell him it's safe for him to come out from behind his log, now.'

'This one is beginning to move,' came Miss Winter's voice, palely, from the other side of the wagon.

'Aye, ma'am,' said Mr Gilfry, 'so I see, thank you. Will! More rope and quick about it!'

Miss Winter was standing over the lieutenant. She was holding his knife in front of her as delicately as she might a hatching egg. He was just beginning to groan and squint against the light.

'I've put his pistols over there,' said Miss Winter, breathlessly. 'They were much heavier than I expected. And look, there is my brother, turning his kaleidoscope, hardly noticing that we have been fighting for our lives.'

And then she laughed, rather wildly.

'Will,' said Mr Gilfry, sharply. 'Hand those pistols to me, boy.'

Will picked them up carefully and handed them to Mr Gilfry, who flicked open a cover, nodded, closed it again, and pulled at a lever. Something clicked, a surprisingly resonant sound, and the lieutenant twitched violently and stopped trying to sit up.

Mr Gilfry handed the pistol carefully back to Will.

'This pistol is loaded and cocked,' he told him. 'That means it's ready to fire. Train it on that man's belly. If he causes any trouble then pull the trigger, here. It'll take him a long time to die, but it's a target you can't miss.'

The lieutenant was a gentleman, a fine officer, but he crawled like anyone else.

'You'd best search his pockets,' said Rosie.

Will put back the handkerchief and the locket and the money; but the penknife he threw deep into a tangle of silvery old man's beard.

Mrs Keen had gone to check on the sergeant. He was still where he'd fallen after Will had pushed him off the top of the load, and gazing peacefully at the pale sky. Mrs Keen looked up as Will and Rosie came round. Her face, usually so warm and full of cheer, had gone saggy and grey. And there was a stillness about her, a weariness, that brought them to a halt.

'This one's cold,' she said. 'Dead and cold.'

Dead? One fewer, then. Good, I make progress. Red-and-orange-and-black-and-blue. Black-and-blue.

She tried with her poison but I was as fast in my shell as a limpet.

And now my world is getting stronger.

Yes, yes, they shall all be dead soon.

Chapter 25

'The ground'll still be frozen too hard to bury him,' said Toby, pacing mournfully round the body.

'He can be made decent, though,' said Mrs Keen. 'Toby! Will! Pull him over to the side of the road out of the way. Rosie, you might stay with young Sam. There's more here than I'd wish him to see.'

The sergeant's head bumped horribly on the ground as they dragged him. Will winced at every knock and twitch of his oily head. A certainty was expanding through him, as cold as the sergeant's flabby hand. *I've killed a man*, he thought, in a circle, over and over again, until it formed a background to everything and was almost lost, but always there, like the whispering of the wind.

Toby helped Mrs Keen take off the sergeant's rucksack. She put it under his head for a pillow, crossed his arms on his breast, weighed closed his eyes with coins from his pocket, and put his handkerchief over his face.

'There,' she said, tugging her pink skirts out from under her knees and heaving herself up. 'That's done. And may he find more peace in death than he knew in life, poor man.'

Will was too frozen inside to speak.

'The sergeant's sabre is Will's, by right,' said Toby.

But Will found he didn't want it. He threw it into the bushes, for at that moment it seemed to him a wicked thing.

'And the *lieutenant's* sabre should be mine,' said Sam. 'For I stole out and undid his horse's girth, and that was what unseated him.' And then, when Rosie turned to look at him, he went on, hastily: 'But I do not want it, either.'

Mrs Keen drew her shawl protectively round her fat shoulders.

'But what shall we find next?' she said, with a shiver. 'Or what shall find *us*? If our own men can treat us so, then what might the enemy do? I still cannot quite believe that we can be so badly used by our friends.'

'They were hardly our friends, Mrs Keen,' said Mr Gilfry.

'Not so you'd notice,' agreed Toby, with just a trace of a chuckle.

'But they wore red coats,' said Sam. 'Red, the King's colour.'

'I suppose,' said Miss Winter, holding on to the side of the wagon as if she really needed its support, 'amongst so many thousands of men there are bound to be some rogues.'

'Aye, ma'am,' said Mr Gilfry, with unusual gentleness. 'And it wasn't their scarlet coats that hurt us, after all, was it.' And he lifted the reins.

The elm hubs turned reluctantly, screeching as

the great blue wagon creaked into motion. Will walked along beside the glossy labouring hindquarters of the horses; and somewhere on the edge of his mind he knew that Toby was holding the ensign's horse for Mrs Keen to mount, and that Miss Winter was being helped, pale but unresisting, onto the sergeant's.

Occasionally, amongst the clop of hooves and the groaning and squeaking of the wagon, Will thought he could hear fragments of glass tumbling round and round in an incomprehensible pattern. He had killed a man.

Rosie was somewhere close.

But he was not sure he was fit even to look at her.

'Twas a long march. We passed, step by step by step, past harvestless fields and hedges studded with titmice. Blackthorn, hazel, hawthorn, elder, hornbeam, elm . . .

Our minds were filled with ugly things that made our feet jar on the ground. So I, the leader, lifted up my voice and sang a song of long ago, of hope.

And our hearts, being joined, lifted with it.

They ate at noon, almost the last of their provisions.

Will took his food away from the rest, and after a long black time he must have dozed. And it was as if it was the morning again, and he was reaching up to Rosie as she sat on the edge of the load. He looked again into Rosie's eyes, bright, but deep as midnight, and he felt again, just for an instant, miraculous, the softness of her skin under his hands. Then there was some alarm—some danger—and he was grasping greedily at her (just warm, her hands were, and fitting so neatly into his own, as if they were meant to be there) and she was flying down to him. And then his arms were full of her: and she was so warm, so solid, so real. And then the cotton of her skirts was slipping up against her petticoats as he held her tight, as tightly as he could. And there was nothing else in the world to wish for, ever, and . . .

It was a bitter awakening.

Distant thunder got them moving again, though they had no idea if there was any shelter ahead. They packed up swiftly and had been walking for a while before they properly realized that the clouds were silver-edged, and that the noise rumbling round the hills did not quite fade into the sulky mumbling that thunder usually did.

It rumbled round the hills about them, somehow not quite like thunder.

'Drums,' said Mr Gilfry, suddenly. 'Those are drums.'

'Where?' asked Toby, turning right round.

Mr Gilfry reined in the horses and they all stared around as the next rumbling swelled menacingly over the grass; but they all looked in different directions.

'The sound bounces off these hills so,' said Mrs Keen.

'I believe there are two sets of drums,' said Miss Winter, hesitantly. 'I am almost sure—'

The master let out a harsh laugh.

'There are, there are! They are symmetrical. And there are echoes, too, reflecting round us. The hills are like a tunnel of mirrors. Yes, it is all coming together.'

The hills rose around them, empty except for a few sodden sheep with neat black legs and roman noses. None of the hill ridges was more than a couple of miles away.

'They may not be able to hear each other,' said Rosie. 'Can we tell if it is two different armies?'

They looked at Mr Gilfry, who had been a soldier, but he shook his head.

'I cannot tell.'

The drums rolled again, and the saddle horses began to shift and tiptoe and roil their eyes.

'Well, we're a sitting duck here,' said Toby, as they turned and twisted round.

'But what can we do?' asked Miss Winter, anxiously shortening her reins. 'What can we do?'

They were so few, and so fragile; and there were armed men just over the ridge. Not just a few men, like that morning, but a whole company, or a brigade, or a regiment: a great sledgehammer of men that could sweep them away as easily as the wind stripped the trees.

Will spoke his thoughts out loud without any consciousness of having formed them.

'We must leave the road,' he said. 'We are a target, here.'

There was a silence as they all took this in.

'But in that case we must turn back,' said Mr Gilfry. 'There is only one bridge, and the river will be flowing high.'

The drums rolled again. Rosie shivered, and pulled her shawl close about her.

'But where can we go?' she asked.

Miss Winter urged her horse forward to stand beside the black spider-shape of the master.

'What should we do?' she asked. 'I need you to tell us. Please tell us. You have always understood how things fitted together. You have always kept us safe.'

'Whilst you were loyal,' said the master, harshly. 'Whilst you knew your place. But not now. Now, I have called the redmen here to finish you.'

Miss Winter's hands must have tightened on the reins, for her horse shied a little, side-stepping nervously away.

'I don't know what to do,' she said to the others. 'I don't know where we should go. I thought I was leading us to safety, but there is no safety. My brother was right. Things keep happening. We try to catch at the good things, but they are swept out of our grasp.'

Mr Gilfry sighed. ''Tis a pity the captain has not been able to find his way back to us, ma'am,' he said gently, 'but in truth a whole platoon of generals would be little protection against the men with those drums.'

'I'm frightened,' said Sam, to no one in particular. 'I'm sorry. I'm sorry. But I'm frightened.'

Rosie gathered him to her in a rush of love, squeezing his pale cheek against her bosoms.

'Oh, Will,' she said, 'what are we to do?'

And Will took a huge breath and let the air blow away his unfitness and his ignorance and his diffidence. He put back his shoulders and gave up all thought of himself altogether. It lifted a burden from him.

'We will go home,' he said. 'We will leave the wagon in the copse, there, and hope it will not be discovered. And then we will follow that sheep-track up over the hill and find our way back to the house from there.'

'But we cannot go back!' said Miss Winter, her voice high with strain. 'Not back to my brother's house. Not to living in the dark, alone. I could not bear it!'

'And we cannot abandon the wagon, surely,' said Mrs Keen. 'Think of all the cutlery. The furnishings. They may be all we possess in all the world.'

'They are not half as valuable as our lives,' said Will.

The others looked at each other.

'But we don't know if we've got a home, Will,' pointed out Toby, rubbing hard at the side of his nose. 'We know there have been rebels riding along the road. We'll be lucky to find anything still standing. All the land round there will be over-run, most likely, and looted and burned.'

'Maybe,' said Will. 'That captain, yesterday, he told us it was bound to happen. But that was partly to frighten us, so we'd welcome his company.'

The rest all moved uneasily, like sheep approached by a strange dog.

'But the captain was deeply concerned about us,' said Miss Winter, though her voice was thin with wretchedness. 'And he could not have been more welcome.'

'Aye, he was a fine man,' said Toby. 'And 'twas only sensible for him to take to his heels when those murdering rebels came along.'

But the world seemed to have fallen into Will's hands: and he looked at it, and he saw it as it was.

'Yes, the captain was a brave handsome soldier,' he said. 'And he certainly spoke fair enough. But he was only after stealing from us. He was more cunning than those we met this morning, but was after the same thing.'

'No,' said Miss Winter, in a gasp of pain.

Mrs Keen stared at Will.

'I'm sure I have no great love for any officer in a scarlet coat,' she said, 'for one took my man away. But you have no reason to say that, Will.'

But Will was suddenly certain. He was sure of everything.

'The captain had his boy stow away our packs while we ate, do you remember? That boy will have been under orders to search through them and take anything valuable.'

Miss Winter's face was white beneath her bonnet, as the blood and hope drained away together.

'But you cannot think . . . he was a King's man,' she said, pleadingly. Then she stopped, and tried again. 'He was an officer . . . '

Toby shook his heavy head.

'I always thought there was something wrong about him,' he said. 'Why, he threw the top of his carrot into the bushes without even asking if it might be wanted. Good compostable stuff. That's a sure sign of a deceitful heart, that is.'

Rosie swung her pack down to the ground and undid the strings with quick fingers.

'Will's right,' she said, flatly, sorting through. 'The silver cruet's gone. And the mistress's amber pendant. And even . . . ' She pulled out a little silken bag that flapped emptily in her fingers. 'Even my little bit of money, too. Every penny of it. Oh, Will . . . '

'I should have known!' exclaimed Mrs Keen, in dawning outrage. 'There we were preening ourselves we were getting stronger, Rosie, when that captain's boy had been through and stole all the mistress's knives and spoons!'

Miss Winter closed her eyes tightly, as if to stop herself seeing what was large and plain in front of her.

'Perhaps the captain did not know . . . ' she began.

'No,' said Mr Gilfry, shaking his great head. 'I'm sorry, ma'am, but they were in it together, sure enough. It was the captain gave orders to have our packs stowed away. I half thought it was strange at the time.'

'A thieving ruffian!' said Mrs Keen, quite wound up. 'And to think I fed him! To think I dropped a tear for him, so handsome as he was, thinking him a brave man and likely to suffer from the fortunes of war, as many a good man does.'

Mr Gilfry snorted.

'There are many fortunes to be made in war, Mrs Keen,' he said, roughly. 'And in many different ways.'

Into the silence that followed his words came a new swelling of drums. Miss Winter's horse plunged forward so powerfully that Sam's feet left the ground for a moment before he was able to pull it up.

Mr Gilfry cracked his mutilated holly whip above the twitching ears of the carthorses.

'Will's right,' he said, with sudden decision. 'We must get away from here, and quickly, for if men are dangerous before a battle, they are madmen afterwards, as I know much too well. We'll make for the copse, as Will said. It'll give us some shelter, perhaps.'

It was not far. Will went ahead and found that a double curve of wheel-carved mud already penetrated deep amongst the trees.

'A timber tug's been here before us, most likely,' said Mr Gilfry, urging the horses on. 'Lead the way, Will.'

Will made his way through the squelching mud between the lines of crushed saplings. At the end was a clearing, and the orange irregular disc that was all that was left of a newly-felled tree. Beech, it had been. It still spread iron-grey fingers into the shallow leaf-litter.

And here, with a screech of axles, and a great huffing and puffing of horses, the wagon was arriving, brave and yellow and blue. Mr Gilfry pulled up the wagon a little short so there would be room to walk the horses forward without getting them tangled in the long pole that held their harness.

'You can still see the wagon from the road,' came Toby's doleful voice, flat in the cold air.

'But I doubt you'd realize what it was, Toby,' said Mrs Keen. 'All this holly breaks up the outline something wonderful.'

The drums came again, loud, and then louder still, and then there was a faint imperious trumpet call—and they were all suddenly struck with fear and haste.

'Get on up the track,' ordered Mr Gilfry. 'You see the white line of it? That's our nearest path, if we're returning. Rosie, you lead the way. Take the right-hand at the fork, and after a mile or so you'll find you can see a stand of pines on your left. Keep it there until you see the monument, and then you'll be able to find your way home from there. Go on, then, girl! Toby, Will, Sam—come help the master down.'

The master was crouched forward into a ball like a starved spider.

'Come, now,' said Will, as gentle as their hurry could be. 'Come, now. We are going to take you back home, master. Back to your tower.'

'Perhaps,' said the master. 'Yes, I shall allow this. The world spins fast, and I must find the centre of it again before it topples.'

They put him on the flea-bitten grey. The master still clutched the kaleidoscope in his white fingers, but when they sat him on the horse and forced his narrow shoes into the stirrups he showed no sign of wanting to throw himself off.

'You'd better walk beside him, Toby, all the same,' said Will.

'Ah well,' said Toby. 'There's nothing like the company of a murderous lunatic to keep your spirits up, is there.'

'And you, Will,' called Mr Gilfry, 'you take the rear, boy. Now, be off with you.'

Rosie was already making her way towards the brightness that must mark the edge of the copse, and Toby was leading the master's horse after her. Mrs Keen was helping Sam with unhitching the great horses. Miss Winter, pale as ice and hardly seeming to know where she was, took the reins of the other horse.

Will hauled himself up onto the wagon with a feeling that this was the last time.

'There's no call to take anything from the load,' said Mr Gilfry, twisting his great bulk round in his seat as far as he could. 'You've enough to carry. Be off with you!'

Will got out his precious knife and began to saw his way through the edge seam of one of the tarpaulins. It was simple, then, to rip off a piece about six feet square.

There were poles stacked by the edge of the clearing, left from the felling of the tree. They were rough, and none too straight, but there were a couple that would do. Will searched in his tool bag for the round beech handle of his bradawl, and some string.

'Take the horses on,' he said to Sam.

Sam moved forward, and the horses, high-stepping disdainfully, stamped the pale turned-over bramble leaves into the mud.

'Mrs Keen!'

'Yes, Will?'

'I'll need your help, if you please, ma'am.'

'Well, here I am, then,' said Mrs Keen.

Will looked up as far as her stout arms and felt surpassingly grateful for them.

Mr Gilfry was still protesting.

'I won't have it,' he said, as Will untied his bath chair, turned it, and, surprised yet again by its unyielding weight, almost tipped Mr Gilfry flat onto the ground far below. 'I'm too heavy, lad. I shall manage here all right. Will, can you not obey an order when it is given to you? If you have any love for me, lad, *leave me here*! I should not want you to put yourself at risk for me. I should not *want* you to.'

'I said I would not leave you,' said Will, doggedly. 'And you would not have me break my word.'

Mrs Keen was stronger even than she looked.

'You don't beat a cake for four hours at a time without getting powerful arms,' she said. 'And I'd be a fool if I've been a cook all these years without seeing myself well fed. Easy does it, now, Will. That's right, Mr Gilfry, you get yourself out of the chair and sit on the raves. Will, you'll have to jump down. That's right. Ready to take his weight, Will? One two *three* . . . There you are, Mr Gilfry, safe on the ground, and we'll soon have you snug as a baby. Now, I'll take the front of the stretcher, Will, for I'm a deal stronger than you, and a great deal tougher. That's it.'

'Are you all right, Mr Gilfry?' asked Will, as they took their first steps with the stretcher. Mr Gilfry was much heavier than Will had imagined. He closed his mind down to all the miles in front of them. Mr Gilfry grunted.

'It's like riding a three-legged camel,' he said, sourly.

'Don't be ungrateful, Mr Gilfry,' said Mrs Keen, but without ill-feeling. 'We're both going to need new sleeves to our clothes after today, Will, for I reckon our arms will reach halfway to our knees. Mind you, Will needs a new coat in any case: the lad grows like a weed.'

Mr Gilfry leaned back and seemed to resign himself to this new humiliation.

'Like a young bull, more like,' he said. 'Strong and wrong-headed, eh, Mrs Keen?'

Sam was waiting for them at the edge of the trees.

'Rosie has taken the horses,' he said, 'so I could wheel the bath chair, if you wanted. We might be able to use it some of the way.'

Will wanted to mop his brow, but there was no way he could do it. He blew up his hair at the front and tried to find words of praise.

'Good lad,' said Mrs Keen. 'A clever thought, that was. I lay we'll be powerful grateful to you before long.'

And Sam's smile lit up the wood like sunshine.

The others were well ahead. Toby was stomping on beside the lop-sided blackness of the master. The women's petticoats were inches deep in mud, though they'd caught up their skirts to keep them as clean as they could.

'Well, then,' said Mrs Keen; and they began the journey up the long hill.

We have been overtaken by many platoons of horsemen, and we have helped to pull out a gun that was stuck in a pothole. *All together, lads!* **I said, needlessly, because everything we do is all together. Months of all-together have made us one.**

The order, passed down from on high, is to bivouac. We are hungry, so I find food. I have to bellow, trudge, near enough fight for it, but I get it in the end.

'This is the life, lads,' I say, sharing and sharing alike. They grin, and half lift their mugs in salutation, but our minds are full of the uncertainty of life, and how little ours might be worth.

Chapter 26

The rough grey poles of the stretcher pulled and twisted in Will's hands, but after the first hundred yards he and Mrs Keen found a rhythm that cushioned them against most of the shocks and jerks. By the end of the second hundred yards the bark had pressed its way fiercely into Will's palms and his shoulders were beginning to cramp; but Mrs Keen's wide pink back was carrying on and on, implacably, and all Will could do was follow, though he felt as if the weight of the stretcher was making him shorter and stockier with each step up the hill.

A cloud of dun-coloured midges came and danced in front of his eyes as sweat formed on his forehead and trickled, ever so ticklishly, into his eyebrows and then down the sides of his face. Sam was tugging the bath chair along beside them, red in the face and almost in tears with the struggle of it.

Will plodded on. Sometimes Mr Gilfry would peer back at him, so he did his best to keep his face from showing his pain. *I will not leave you*, Will had said: well, now he had to keep his word.

Here was the top of the rise at long last. Mrs Keen's massive behind was swaying on and on in front of him, but surely when they reached the top she would stop to rest. Surely. The others would be waiting for them, and perhaps Toby would take a turn with the stretcher. Will would lead the master's horse, he would, and without a single worry for its hard brown hooves and yellow teeth.

They topped the rise. The track petered out here and the grass dipped; but then—oh, but then it rose on up again, higher and higher, shouldering its way up over the short chalk grass further than Will could see. And the others were far ahead, walking without a thought for the three of them struggling behind.

Will could not keep his face from twisting in bitterness and weakness and disappointment.

'Stop, now,' ordered Mr Gilfry. 'Sam, leave that chair and go and catch up with the others as quickly as you can. Tell them we need help. Put me down for a little while, if you please, Mrs Keen, Will. Thank you kindly.'

Will's hands had been gripping the poles so long that it took two or three attempts before he could get them to let go of them.

'Well, we've maybe come a mile,' said Mrs Keen, waggling her big shoulders and rubbing her hands gingerly on her skirts, 'and that all uphill. I think we shall get you home, Mr Gilfry, though I doubt my hands will be fit for rolling piecrust for a day or two.'

Will's arms and legs were shaking. He walked away so the others shouldn't see. The shaking got worse as he went, until his knees were locking and buckling and threatening to let him down.

There was a thorn tree, here, stunted and slanted back against the hillside away from the wind. It was naked now apart from a few shuddering lemon leaves, and it gave no shelter to speak of, but there was a small stump there. Will allowed his legs to fold, let his head hang down over his knees, and enjoyed the ultimate luxury of stillness and rest.

He was roused by the drums. From up here they sounded thinner, like a rattle. Will looked up and all his shoulder muscles yelped and protested, for he'd gone as stiff as a badly-jointed doll.

'Will!'

That was Rosie's voice. She was coming up behind him. She was saying something, but Will was not listening, did not even turn to look at her, though she was as close to him as she'd ever been, not even though she was putting her hand on his shoulder and leaning forward to gaze into his face.

The plain below him was streaked and blotched with colour. Before it had been all grey grass, and scars of dirty chalk, and the long streak of mud and hedges that was the road; but now there were lines of red, and green, and squares of blue, as if someone had arranged coloured bricks on the grass. And as he looked Will saw that the lines and squares were moving, though it seemed to him as though they were moving very slowly, because they were so far away. Sometimes there was a speck of light, perhaps reflecting off metal, and sometimes a line would begin to bulge and move more quickly and reveal itself to consist of horsemen. And there, there was a team of four horses: yes, look, that long lurching cylinder must be a cannon. Will had never seen one, but George had told him all about them. They fired a ball that might weigh twenty-five pounds—though those were the siege-pieces, that stayed fixed on the walls of cities. These were leaner, perhaps nine-pounders, but they might have the greater range for all that.

Will's heart beat fast. Here was a battle forming, just as he had heard about. Somewhere there would be a general with a plumed hat so all his men could see him. He and the enemy general would have plans, very clever plans, to outfox each other and win a glorious victory.

'Will,' said Rosie, again; and it was only then that he realized properly that she was there. He grabbed her arm in pure excitement.

'Look,' he said. 'See, Rosie? It is to be a battle, I'm sure of it, just there below us.'

'Yes,' said Rosie, in a curiously flat voice. 'That's what it looks like, sure enough.'

Will watched as the lines and squares moved, slowly, so slowly, and he felt as if he almost had the key to what was going on, as if he was almost like a general himself.

'We are ready to move on, Will,' said Rosie.

Will looked up at her, and all his aches and pains had vanished in his great excitement.

'There is going to be a battle,' he said, again; and his whole face was beaming at her.

'That's right,' said Rosie.

Will could not understand why she was not shining with excitement, too. He turned back to watch the shifting shapes below.

'It is like the kaleidoscope,' he said, feeling suddenly almost greedy, though he did not know for what. 'All those colours, and shapes. That is what it is like. Look! Look, see, Rosie? That big flag. That will be their colours, as they call them. It is special to the men, the colours are. I've heard tell that the men would gladly die rather than let the colours be taken.'

'And why is that, Will?' asked Rosie, still quietly, still with that flat sound to her voice.

'Because—it is a matter of honour, Rosie. That's what they say. They would be shamed by it. Soon the generals will have all their men set out, and the guns, too, and then they will have their men attack. Look! Look, see those muskets? See how extra long they are? They have fixed their bayonets. That makes the muskets heavy, that does, and the men have to take great care when they are using their ramrods, not to slice their hands. George told me all about it. Infantryman's hand, they call it, on account of how easy it is to do.'

Rosie gave a sudden deep shudder.

'We need you, Will,' she said. 'Toby and Sam are going to pull Mr Gilfry in his bath chair, but they aren't strong enough to carry the stretcher far if the ground gets too rough for the chair.'

The image of Mr Gilfry made a splodge of dullness on the edge of the glorious brightness in front of Will's eyes, but he ignored it.

'If I ran down the slope I could help in the battle,' he said. 'I could help with loading the cannon, perhaps, or I could give the men their dinner.'

'And which side would you help, Will?' asked Rosie, still in that tired, quiet voice that was so unlike herself.

'Oh, I wouldn't mind,' said Will. 'And then, when the fighting started, if a man was hurt—so he couldn't fight—then I could take over his musket. I know what to do, George told me all about it. You have to bite off the end of the cartridge, see, and—'

There was a puff of smoke from one of the guns, and it jerked backwards. And then, a curiously long time afterwards, there came the empty explosion. Where the ball went was anybody's guess, for everything carried on as before, but now under faint curlicues of drifting blue smoke.

'And who would you kill?' asked Rosie.

'The enemy. We'd be in files, two with muskets, two with bayonets. You pick out your man, and then you wait until the officer gives the order to fire. A musket has a range of eighty yards, and a man can run that in just a few seconds, easy, let alone a horse, so you have to look sharp. A rifle, that can fire two hundred and fifty yards, but they're slower to load on account of the rifling in the barrel. But then, the riflemen have swords that they can fix to their rifles instead of bayonets: and that would be fine, to have a sword.'

Rosie came and stood in front of him, blocking his view.

'And then you would have killed another man,' she said. 'What a fine thing that would be. You know, when the sergeant died this morning I was afraid to look at him. And the same with the dead man by the side of the road yesterday. You were shielding him from my sight, and so I walked past not knowing what a splendid sight I was missing. I thought in my foolishness that it would be a dreadful thing, enough to give me nightmares. But instead I should have taken Sam by the hand and showed him. *Look*, I should have said, *look at this man with all his insides spilling out like chitterlings. Look at the big brave scarlet sergeant with his head at such a funny angle. See how clever and wonderful men can be.* And if I'd done that, then perhaps Sam would have been even sharper to look for a chance to run away and join in all the fun, and get his insides spilled in the mud.'

More drums sounded, a ruffle mounting to a rattle and then to a snarl and away again. And then there was a trumpet, a bright trumpet-call that split the dull air into splinters of brilliance. Will's heart leapt at the sound of it: he wanted to follow it, to be part of the brightness below him, to follow the colours that tumbled in the wind just as the colours in the kaleidoscope tumbled.

He looked up at Rosie, and the sight of her stabbed him with a terrible pain, as if his heart was wrenched into two; and he knew he was poised, balanced, between one loss and another.

'Mr Gilfry needs you, Will,' said Rosie, soberly. 'And I need you, too.'

And the brightness sparkling around him winked and faded, and he found himself on a grey hillside below a wind-torn sky.

He pushed himself wearily to his feet.

'I'm coming,' he said. And he began the long walk back towards the others.

Trumpets, and we advance, together. Someone falls, but we hold on to the strength of the rest of us and we do not falter. I am proud of that.

Another man spins and jerks and falls, but we are roaring, roaring, and thrusting our bayonets at the enemy. All around, dark in the blue smoke, are dancing, striving, writhing figures, for this is the moment when each heart beats to the same rhythm.

And then a breeze blows, and the smoke shreds into fleeting wisps like ghosts.

And there, yawning at our feet, are the mouths of destruction.

Chapter 27

The way home over the hills was much shorter than by the road, but darkness found them floundering at a crossroads. The deep mud squelched and squirted and spattered hems and stockings. They had no water, nor food, nor anywhere to rest.

'We cannot stop here,' said Miss Winter. She sounded close to exhaustion, perhaps close to tears. 'We will wait until the moon comes up, and then we must go on.'

'Aye, ma'am,' said Mr Gilfry. 'We should be back at the house in another couple of hours of walking.'

Will was surrounded by people who were only shadows, but still amazingly recognizable by the way they moved.

'If the house is still there,' said Toby, dourly.

Rosie shivered.

'How can it be that nowhere is safe?' she asked. 'We only want to live at peace. That isn't much to ask.'

'There is no peace,' said Miss Winter, bleakly. 'None to be found anywhere. The only peace lies in turning away from the world, or in turning away from oneself; and my brother has done one, and I the other. What a waste it has been, to have thrown away all my youth. But I shall sacrifice no more years, whatever happens; not even for the sake of peace.'

There was a silence except for the faint jingling of harnesses.

'Look!' said a harsh voice. It was so long since it had spoken that everybody jumped. 'The moon, the hunters' moon!'

'Yes, sir,' said Will. 'It is the moon.'

'It slides along very smoothly,' said the master. 'It is clever and lights up only a little of the world. A streak here, a jagged path there. Sensible, sensible. For the world is not in order yet.'

'There,' said Mrs Keen. 'There is a hopeful thought, then, that the world will get back to how it should be, and we shall have our proper places back.'

'It is hardly a thought at all,' said Miss Winter. 'It is not much more than a dream. And we have already wasted too much of our lives in dreams.'

The kaleidoscope draws everything in.
> *Into the pattern.*
> *Blue grey white black.*
> *Red.*

Chapter 28

They came home in the grey dawn, under the archway and into the courtyard. Sam squeaked in dismay at the coppery corpses that were all the fox had left of the hens.

'Well,' sighed Mrs Keen, 'we shall have a fine dinner or two from these, at the least.'

Everything of value had been abandoned with the wagon, but still the house seemed full of comfort. It was there, after all. There were beds with mattresses a thousand times softer and warmer than the muddy ground; there were tables to eat from; even a dish of broth seemed a luxury.

They fed the master and helped him to his bed, and then they all slept themselves, careless of dirt, or the first thumps of the morning's cannon-fire in the distance. Will slept like a log until noon, and awoke to the far-away rumbling of the battle; and he brought to mind the bright squares and lines of the two armies swirled up in their dance of honour.

Mr Gilfry was grey-faced on the bed that Will had made for him in the scullery.

'Leave me here a while, Will,' he said. 'All the

journeying has felled me, for now. I shall be up and about again presently.'

Will took in a breath of foreboding.

'What's wrong, Mr Gilfry? Is there anything I can do?'

Mr Gilfry shook his great grizzled head.

'No, no, I shall get on well enough. Now off you go, boy, there'll be lots that needs to be done.'

But Will still hesitated.

'Can I come in when I need help, Mr Gilfry?'

'Yes, you must do that, Will. Don't worry, boy. I shall not leave you to fend for yourself, any more than you left me.'

Red. Yes, that has been good, very good, for blood, for destruction. Very good, indeed. But here is green. Green, for rebellion—which is destructive, too. Green, now, shall play its part.

Yes.

Sam was white with tiredness, but he was up and grooming the horses.

'I'm going to take them up to the high field,' he said. 'I reckon they are least likely to be discovered there, if soldiers come.'

Will ruffled up the hair at the back of his neck. He could not think of anywhere better. In fact, he could not *think*, at all. He felt as if he were in the tower looking down on everybody; as if all the people were pieces of glass from the kaleidoscope, and he could no more understand what they were doing than he could understand the bits of glass.

Sam was rubbing one of the horses over with a wisp of hay. It was the sergeant's horse, a strange horse, and yet it stood contentedly and even reached round to nuzzle Sam's neck as he worked.

'You're a good lad,' said Will. 'But come back as soon as you've finished. Rosie will want to know that you are safe.'

He walked round past the barn and into the garden. He followed the sound of a doggedly-driven spade until he saw Toby's round backside labouring at the huge soft mounds of the dung-heaps.

'How shall we hide the women, if soldiers come?' asked Will, abruptly.

Toby looked up at the windows of the house. Then he sniffed violently, and shook his head.

'Don't ask me. Miss Winter, she knows the house best, I suppose. She might know of somewhere. Mind you, now she's decided to make up for lost time, it's maybe not only the soldiery that'll be doing the chasing, poor mare.'

'It's not a joke,' said Will, surprising himself by the sharpness of his tone.

Toby glared back at him.

'I know it's not,' he said. 'I know we saw off those three men yesterday by good fortune and nothing else. If there'd been four of them we couldn't have. And if they'd decided to shoot us, then that'd have been that. So what *can* we do but jest, or pretend none of it's going to happen? To tell the truth, I'm beginning to think the master might be as sensible as any of us.'

Will thought of Rosie, hiding, frightened, in some dark attic, while outside soldiers took whatever they wanted.

And he thought of the Red House.

It was enough to make even breathing difficult.

'What if they set the place afire?' he asked.

'Don't ask me,' said Toby, again. 'There's no answer. I know my dung-heap, that's all.'

'But—'

'There's nothing we can do,' said Toby, suddenly, almost angrily. 'Nothing, save to get away and make new lives for ourselves and leave behind all that we hold dear: that, or tell the men where the women are and let them take what they want.'

Will shook his head.

'There must be a better way than that.'

'In war? Well then, Will, you be sure to tell me when you discover what it is.'

Chapter 29

We had no chance. Not one, not the smallest. Behind the smoke the pattern of the battle had changed. Around us were a thousand of the enemy, and there were only a score of us still standing.

It was bitter to know this was the end for us, for every part of us. Here was a force like a forest fire that would leave nothing behind it: not sapling youth as fine as willow, nor sturdy beech, nor aged gnarled oak; hair of teak, deal, chestnut, ebony, all ashes, ashes . . .

There was a block of ebony in the barn at home. Goodness knows where it had come from, but it was as heavy as stone and even my father could not shift it.

I seemed to smell the sawdust of the barn. It was not my home, not now, but it might still be my refuge. I, with my men, my comrades, my brothers, would be stronger than the others. And that, at last, is all that counts.

I led my men away: it was not glorious, but it was that, or death.

We went together.

They heard trumpets as the day was turning blue with dusk. Will and Toby met in the courtyard again on their way to the kitchen.

'They're a fair way off,' said Will. 'On the road. Ten to one they'll ride past.'

Toby hunched his shoulders apprehensively.

'Ten to one, do you think? Because the last nine companies rode past. And you heard what Mr Gilfry said: men go mad after a battle. They'll be raping and murdering and thieving . . . and they're coming, this lot, aren't they?'

Will shook his head. How should he know?

'Look, I'm off,' said Toby, suddenly. 'I'm sorry about the dunghill, for it breaks my heart to leave it, but I'm going into the woods, I am. There's a charcoal burner's hut I know. No soldiers will find that.'

'No,' said Will. 'Don't go. We need you here.'

Toby glowered at him.

'But you *don't*,' he growled. 'Me being here's not going to be any help if we get overrun, is it? What's the point in us all getting killed?'

'I don't know why we need you,' said Will, a little wildly, 'but you must be better than nothing!'

'We'll just all get killed,' said Toby, walking round in a circle and scratching his head. Then he stopped, and a moment later Will became aware of another rumbling far away.

Toby's eyes bulged most of the way out of his head.

'Those are more horses,' he said, exasperated

and outraged. 'A whole company of them, at least. We can't do anything against that lot if they come here. Let's go, Will. Together. I'll show you that hut. I don't mind sharing. We can look out for each other.'

And now there was someone running in under the archway.

Sam could hardly speak from breathlessness.

'They're coming,' he said. 'There are rebels coming along the road, hundreds of them. Where's Rosie?'

But he was running across to the kitchen door before Will could make any answer.

Toby stood and stared at Will. And then all his haste gradually drained away until he seemed even heavier, almost peaceful in his deep gloom.

'Well, we're done for, now,' he said, quite simply. 'I've turned my last compost heap, I have. Still, I suppose it's been a good life. There aren't many people who've been able to dedicate themselves to a cause like I have.'

Will made himself breathe down the panic that was expanding in his belly. Will Nunn. That was all he was: Will *nothing*. What could he do if soldiers came here?

Everything he could, that was all.

'Mind you, I wish I'd had a chance to make a hot-bed and grow some melons,' said Toby, wistfully.

Will made for the house.

Will went from grey room to grey room. He shouted the women's names, but there was no answer, and he began to wonder if he was in a dream.

Another troop of horses were galloping along

the road. They came to the end of the drive and Will held his breath; but then they were past, and galloping away again.

Will called again; and this time there was an answer. He ran up the black pinnacled staircase and found Sam jogging along the corridor towards him.

'Where has everybody gone?' asked Will.

'They've vanished,' said Sam.

Will stared at him.

'But how—where—'

'I don't know. I don't know, Will. Rosie . . . she's gone and didn't tell me. I've looked for her everywhere, but . . . '

Sam had to stop to wipe his nose on his sleeve.

'They probably heard the horses and decided they'd best hide,' said Will. 'Most probably they had no time to find you, Sam. Or me,' he finished up, as steadily as he could.

'But where are they, Will?'

Will shook his head and began to lead Sam back to the stairs.

'The fewer of us that know that, Sam, the safer they will be.'

Through the bones of the great window the trees turned and swayed their scratchy fingers against the sky. And with the gusting of the wind there came a new noise: the tramping beat of many hobnailed boots. And it was close, close: on the drive.

Will's first impulse was to dive in among the bits of wood and dusty sacking in the cupboard under the tower stairs. He could hide there for hours, for a day even. He could steal out after dark and get water and food—or sneak out and away and make a new life. A new life, with a new name, even, but with more knowledge than foolish Will Nunn had ever had.

A new life without Sam, without Mr Gilfry, without Rosie.

'Will!' said Sam, beside him, waveringly. 'Will!'

Will swallowed hard, and gripped Sam's shoulder.

'You stay with me, Sam,' he said. 'I shall look after you.'

And he stood and watched and waited for whatever was coming.

The blackness of the archway deepened, moved, as if some giant beast was stirring there: and then it was spewing out men, soldiers, in grimy green uniforms, with their grey blanket-rolls on their backs and their muskets in their hands. Twenty of them, there must have been: so many, so many.

Their leader was only a young man, a corporal, but he was broad in the shoulders and he carried himself proudly.

The corporal gave the word to halt. He looked round the darkening courtyard and up at the silver windows of the house.

And Will, with a feeling as though a chilly waterfall was running through him, stared, openmouthed, as the whole world spun around him into a new pattern.

For it was George.

Chapter 30

''Tis George!' shouted Sam, and ran back along the landing in a clatter of boots. 'Rosie! Rosie! 'Tis George, 'tis George! He has come home!'

Will steadied himself as best he could. It was George. He took in a deep breath and ran back down the stairs, pulled open the great door at the end of the hallway and went out. He stepped into a silence as complete and tight as the world's end. He froze, stock-still. He was under the steely gaze of sixty eyes—and a dozen of them belonged to the muskets that were pointing at his chest.

George took four long strides towards Will, and as his boots thudded on the cobbles Will's world faded, faded, until it became muted and grey.

'Will Nunn,' said the corporal, amazed, in a well-remembered voice: and it was a shock to Will to discover how much he disliked that voice. 'Will Nunn, a head and a half taller, and a great deal wider. I really have been away a long time, haven't I?'

Will found himself ducking his head. This was George: George, the clever one, the heir to Mr Gilfry's craft, the daring hero.

His friend.

The rebel.

Rosie's sweetheart.

'Well?' said George. 'Are you not going to bid me welcome, Will?'

'Of—of course,' stammered Will. 'Welcome, George.' But his voice squeaked as he forced out the words in a way that it had not done for ages.

George looked up again at the windows of the silent house.

'How many of you are there left here? Toby's still here, I've no doubt. I wager he felt no call to go to war. But Jack? Giles? James?'

'All left long since, George,' said Will. 'And not returned.'

George looked round consideringly.

'Where's my father?'

Will, shivering in cold bewilderment, found himself trying to duck under his own words.

'I'm afraid he has had an accident, George. He's fallen off the ladder, and broken his leg.'

George grunted.

'And here I am come through a war with hardly a scratch to my name.' He looked round again through the violet dusk.

'It is a great while since I was here, but it all looks much the same. I expect my father will have sprouted a few more white hairs, and the master will have got even more crazed, if that is possible, up there in his tower. But where are the womenfolk? Hiding away from the soldiers, are they?'

Will's mouth opened very slowly because he

did not know what he was going to say. But he did not have to say anything, for there were footsteps, light running footsteps, from the direction of the kitchen garden.

No, breathed Will; but he could not stop the steps running on.

Rosie burst into the courtyard. She was flushed, and her bosom was heaving.

'George!' she exclaimed. 'Oh, George, I have missed you. I thought you were dead. I did. I had given you up long—'

And then she caught sight of the wide green circle of men behind him, and she faltered to a stop.

George looked her up and down appraisingly, and Will wanted to punch his face.

'And I have missed you, Rosie, certainly,' George said; but he was already looking behind her.

Mrs Keen came and stood at Rosie's shoulder. She smiled at George, but her eyes were wary.

'And a corporal, too, coming back at the head of a troop just as Will always said you would,' she said. 'Why, this will do your father's heart good, George.'

Miss Winter had come too, but she stayed in the shadow of the wall, as pale as a wraith, her eyes slipping in horror from one green figure to another.

'It is George, ma'am,' said Rosie. 'Back from the wars!'

'Yes,' said Miss Winter, shrunken behind her apprehensive eyes. 'But . . . I did not know—'

Rosie and Mrs Keen began talking loudly at the same time.

'George has been caught up in great matters, ma'am.'

'I'm sure we cannot hope to understand the wrongs and rights of it all, ma'am.'

George grinned whitely through the indigo shadows.

'Very great matters,' he said. 'It's strange to think of, isn't it, that I can leave here the carpenter's boy and come back the master of the house.'

Miss Winter clutched the material of her jacket fearfully to her throat and her lips moved, as if to say *master*?

'Aye,' said George, calmly. 'You see, it's a simple question of science. Of forces. Like this.'

He raised a hand, and the muskets in his men's hands swung down to the horizontal once more.

George looked round searchingly at all their white frozen faces; and, then, satisfied, he lowered his hand and the muskets went back to the rest position.

Rosie moved forward a little.

'George,' she said, hesitantly, 'you must have seen so many terrible things. But you are back home, now. You can rest. There is no need to fight any more.'

That amused the men. The harsh edge of a chuckle passed round them and petered out in the stone cube of the courtyard.

'I am back, now, Rosie, certainly,' said George. But his eyes travelled away from her and back to the outside world.

* * *

Will needed to go away, to be still, to think: he felt as if he were shrinking, and he was terribly afraid he was going to disappear completely. He went away quietly, unnoticed, to be alone; but here was Sam, who had followed him into the darkness of the barn.

'Will!'

Will sat himself down on a stool. The world was spinning round him so fast that he needed the security of something solid underneath him.

Sam came and leaned against Will's shoulder so that Will could not help but put his arm round him.

'Will, what if George wants to know where the horses are?'

Sam smelt of oats and hay. An honest, reassuring smell.

'I think you must tell them that the soldiers took them,' said Will, slowly.

Sam frowned, but then nodded.

'It isn't true,' he said. 'not really, but . . . '

Will squeezed Sam's arm, trying to impart a comfort that he did not feel himself.

'You're too young to understand these things, yet, Sam,' he said. 'You go to Rosie—' but then he caught himself up short. Rosie. Rosie, George's sweetheart.

Again, the world tumbled dazzlingly round Will, even though the barn was filled with charcoal shadows.

Rosie was clever, was kind: she would not side against them. Not even with George. Not even though George had a place in the world, which was what she had always wanted.

'Will?' whispered Sam.

'Go to Mrs Keen, Sam. She will need help. And stay with her, do you understand? Rosie . . . Rosie will be busy.'

'But can't I stay with you?'

Will pushed himself to his feet.

'I must be busy too,' he said.

Chapter 31

'What's happening, Will?' asked Mr Gilfry, queru-lously, helpless and abandoned on his bed in the dark scullery. 'I heard tramping feet and voices. There are soldiers come, aren't there?'

Will stood in the doorway and again he was aware that everything had changed. This was George's father, and George's master, too: but Mr Gilfry was also a cripple, and no longer young.

Will could not tell him the truth. Indeed, he could not be sure what was the truth and what was fear and jealousy and darkness.

'Yes, Mr Gilfry. About twenty of them.'

'And was that George's voice I heard?'

Will made himself smile, though Mr Gilfry would not be able to see it.

'Yes, indeed, he has come home, Mr Gilfry. He is made corporal, with all the men under his com-mand. He asked after you, almost the first thing, he did. But he is busy, naturally, just at the moment.'

Will could feel Mr Gilfry's eyes on him, could feel the doubt that did not dare to expand into joy and thankfulness.

'And how is he, Will?'

'Much taller and stouter. And he has grown a moustache. A fine well-set-up man, Mr Gilfry.'

Mr Gilfry shifted restlessly on his bed.

'You are a good lad,' he said, 'but a man does not come straight home from victory, and he does not bring a troop with him when he does . . . Where are the women? And young Sam?'

Outside there was an extra kerfuffle of loud feet, and then shouts and a scuffling; and then there was a strange sound, like the whining of a wounded dog. Or perhaps that was a word, repeated over and over again: *no no no no no* . . .

Mr Gilfry threw back his cover, was confronted by his splinted leg—and then put up his hands to cover his face. It was as if he was daunted, Will saw with horror, as if Mr Gilfry was not the strongest person in the whole world.

'All this going on, Will,' he said. 'I cannot bear to think on it. All this, and here I am, useless.'

'No,' said Will. 'No. Why . . . why, if you were not here, I should not have courage to do anything.'

He had almost said, *you are like a father to me*. But Mr Gilfry did not need him for a son any more. And Rosie would not need him either: not for anything.

Will Nunn, he was, just as he had always been. The world had tumbled him into the light, and then back into the twilight again, for every revolution ends where it begins. Will Nunn: Will Nothing. Like an ant picked up on a cartwheel: swooping up, up, up, and then down again, and crushed to nothing.

The whining outside was going on and on, nerve-scraping, unbearable.

Mr Gilfry sighed again.

'Go and see what is happening, Will,' he said.

There was something on the ground in the middle of the courtyard. Light flickered fitfully, now, from every window of the house, but the something was surrounded by a thicket of legs and Will could not see what it was. He went quietly across the cobbles so he could look over the men's shoulders.

'We found him in his bed,' a dark figure was saying. 'He fought like a cat when we laid hands on him.'

Will could see the something better, now. He could see a scrawny ankle poking out from a thing like a black spider, like a collapsed tripod, like a bundle of sticks. And there, there, against the golden humps of the cobbles, was a sharp elbow, and a ruffle of grey lace, and a straggle of greasy hair.

It was moaning, piteously.

'Let me see him, then.'

Hands grabbed the man on the cobbles and pulled him round. He came all of a piece, as if he was carved of wood, almost too light for a man. Will was confronted by a bleached limewood face, its eyes squeezed shut behind the twiggy cover of its fingers. It still clutched the kaleidoscope.

Will couldn't help but recoil. The face was so full of fear and vicious churning hate, and the body was so frail. He felt a terrible revulsion, and a terrible pity.

George stared at it steadily. He was tall and full of health, the absolute opposite of the poor creature in front of him.

'This is the master of the house,' he said. 'Once, I doffed my cap to him. But that, lads, was in the old days.'

There was a cheer, or perhaps a jeer, and Will found himself surrounded by jostling lamp-hewn faces.

But then, horribly, the spider-figure spoke.

'You are not real,' it said, in a shrill, harsh voice. 'You are not part of the pattern. You are only an edge of the poison: a shadow, a nightmare.'

George smiled, a little ruefully, and shook his head.

'It's lucky we have no need of a master any more,' he said. 'Especially this poor old mad one. For we're turning ourselves a better world, lads, aren't we?'

There was a proper cheer, this time, and Will felt his heart lift irresistibly, stupidly, with those around him.

'But there's work to do for now,' said George. 'Duty for a while, until all is secure. Tidy him away.'

They carried the master out of the courtyard and across the drive and threw him into the glittering muddy margins of the pond. The master gave out a sharp howl as the water hit him, but then sat as he landed, a bundle of twitching bones, with the white ripples spreading round. Will stood in the shadows, shivering, as the old order of the house faded absolutely with the rings of light.

In the strange new world George was giving orders for sentries and dinner and sleeping. Will waited quietly, and when the men had gone back to the house he went out under the archway and very carefully helped the twisted creature which had been the master out of the water. Will stripped him, and washed him down; and then Will dried him with his own shirt and put his jacket around the man's scrawny shoulders.

'This seems so real, so real,' muttered the master. 'Like a whirlpool. It seeks to suck me in. I thought . . . oh, but perhaps there are other crafts-men in the world, and our patterns are colliding! What then? What then?'

Will took him by the hand and led him to Mr Gilfry. The master came quietly enough, like a child, but shaking and still muttering.

'I do not know how to help him,' said Will. Mr Gilfry sighed.

'He has retreated far from us,' he said. 'And if he will not be reached, he cannot be helped, Will.'

'What should we do? Shall I fetch Miss Winter?'

Mr Gilfry shook his head.

'We none of us have much to offer him, just now, even if we could coax him back to us,' he said. 'And I do not think his sister has the will to try any more. He is best where he is. And I swear to you,

Will, I wish I could be with him: for defeat is uglier even than victory, and, oh, I have such memories of victory . . . Oh, Will, how can I forget what I have seen, felt, done, in times like these?'

'I wish I knew,' said Will.

Mr Gilfry sighed.

'Let the master stay here with me for the night. Bring the old dog's bed in from the barn, and a blanket or two: that'll give him comfort, perhaps.'

Mr Gilfry was holding a cup of water to his master's lips when Will returned.

'There,' said Mr Gilfry, with gruff gentleness. 'There is a bed for you, man. You can be alone there.'

The crooked man curled himself up on it, clutching the blankets so they covered his chalky face.

'There, he'll sleep, now, perhaps,' said Mr Gilfry. 'And when it is daylight he'll look at his telescope, again, I expect, turning it this way and that. It seems to bring him comfort.'

'It is a kaleidoscope,' said Will.

Chapter 32

Will left Mr Gilfry and went into the shadowy house. He blundered round the corridors, bumping into walls and doors like a dazzled moth. He needed to find Rosie, but he was both dizzy with the tumbling of the world and in real physical pain at the thought of her, of George, of them together, so he felt as if one of George's muskets had lodged a bullet in the guts.

But still, however the house spun round him, he could not think of stopping till he found her.

He stumbled down the last empty corridor of the house and out into the hugeness of the night.

He knew where the others were: Miss Winter was on her uncurtained bed, weeping for fear the men would batter their way in through her locked door, and for shame that they would not. Toby was down in the kitchen with Mrs Keen and Sam. Toby was weeping too, great swollen sobs of hurt that made his fat cheeks judder. Some of the men had had some sport with him. He had proved entertaining, and his pride and bones were bruised almost to breaking point.

'Will?'

Will's heart somersaulted as a whisper came out of the darkness at his elbow.

Rosie. Here was Rosie. Here, alone. Rosie.

Her figure was invisible in the darkness.

'Will,' she breathed. 'What are you doing out here?'

He could smell her. If he had put out his hand he could have touched her, felt her warmth rise through his skin in a tide.

He hurriedly put away all those thoughts.

'I wanted . . . a bit of peace and quiet,' he said, for there was no foothold to be found on the truth any more, not while everything was spinning so fast.

He could just make out the shine of her eyes, and the doubtful tilt of her head.

'George has men stationed all round the house,' she said. 'Inside and out. It's dangerous out here, Will.'

Will knew that; and he also knew that George, knowing the house well, had made an exceptionally good job of positioning his men.

'I'll do well enough,' he said. But her eyes were glittering at him, searching and intelligent.

'You are not leaving, Will? You are not leaving Sam and Mr Gilfry and the others?'

He shook his head.

She tried to look into his face, but he kept in the shadows.

'Well, I must leave,' she whispered; and Will's heart jumped clumsily inside him—mostly with alarm, but perhaps with some struggling hope.

'But Rosie—'

She looked at him and her wide frozen eyes shone bluely in some stray streak of light.

'You know I must leave, Will. George—George will have come back for me, as well as for other things.'

'Yes,' whispered Will, not even trying to think what she might mean. 'Of course he has. He said he would. And he's a fine man, now, Rosie, with a position and men to serve him, just as you deserve.'

She leaned forward so that her warm breath touched his cheek.

'Help me to get away, Will,' she whispered, and her words were jerky with fright; or so he would have said, if this had not been Rosie. 'Please. Because I don't . . . I don't want George any more.'

And then the world was juddering round again, so Will could not think, though it was desperately important that his head was as clear and strong as when he moved his chisel to the spinning lathe. George had come back, handsome and powerful and successful, and Rosie—and Rosie wanted to leave the house, which meant going out into the tumbling disordered world of thousands of men at war.

'But where could you go?' he asked, clutching at one part of the problem as it cartwheeled past his eyes. 'There is such danger, Rosie, out there.'

Her breath was uneven with apprehension.

'I might not be noticed,' she said. 'I might find somewhere. Nothing can protect me here.'

Will shivered. It was impossible that Rosie should set out into the turmoil of the world outside the house: except that she was right, the turmoil had come right to them. It was churning round in their bellies, in their heads, a mash of filth and fear and diamonds, even though Rosie was only a speck of dust in the vastness of the cosmos.

'What of the other women?' he asked. 'Miss Winter, and Mrs Keen?'

'Mrs Keen says she is done with running. She admits defeat. She says that all the world is gone mad, and that fate can run faster than she can.'

'And Miss Winter?'

'Miss Winter will not open her door to me. She does not trust me. She thinks that George and I . . . I have tried and tried; but oh, Will, I dare not stay any longer!'

Will tried to think, but all the colours of his world were fading round him so he could not see. So he thought about Rosie, who would take with her a small patch of brightness, even if it was out of his sight. It was some tiny scrap of comfort.

'Well,' he said, as calmly as he could. 'I'd best help you get away, then.'

Will stilled himself and listened hard to the sounds of the night. There was a great lumping ox of a trooper stationed at the corner of the house, but he was smoking a pipe and could be tracked by the surprisingly visible trail of grey smoke that rose against the sky. There was another man stationed under the archway—but the box hedge had grown two inches in the year that George had been gone, and it was now high enough to give cover to someone crawling past on hands and knees.

'Are you ready?' said Will, softly, to the scented darkness beside him.

'I'm ready, Will.'

He wanted to hold her properly for one first, one last time; but he was afraid that if he did that he would never let go of her.

'We had best not talk any more, then,' he said, with a hundred things on his tongue that he'd never dared say.

'Very well, Will.'

'Now, then . . . '

There was a smear of mist just settling on the grass, but hardly enough to conceal a mouse. Will loped gingerly across the damp flagstones of the path and down behind a statue of a lady with only a shawl clutched round her frozen skin. A moment later Rosie was beside him. He felt the draught of her coming blow against his cheeks, but he'd been aware only of his own footsteps. He wanted to say *good*, to smile, to touch her arm, but he didn't dare. He stayed still, crouching, taking in deep careful breaths, turning his head away and down so the steam from his nostrils would not be visible to the trooper twenty yards across the grass.

Will pointed to the great urn that stood at the end of the hedge. There was just enough light to see the dead sprouts of the weeds that erupted skinnily from it. Will counted the ten slow steps of the soldier's beat, the stamping as he paused, and then the first step of the walk back again. Then Will ran.

It was only a few seconds' run, but it was out in the open and he expected every gust of wind to herald a bullet. He got to the urn, threw himself past it and onto the ground, and a moment later Rosie fell half on top of him. Will lay still, clutching at the cold grass, trying not to think too much about Rosie's warm body as she rolled away from him. He must concentrate on getting his bearings again, on planning their next move, but it was hard to believe that anything was solid or real when everything was shifting, shifting, with every passing second. He began to crawl as noiselessly as possible, and the long shadow of the hedge draped itself over him.

Rosie, usually so brisk and business-like, was moving almost completely silently. They were at the end of the hedge before he heard any distinct sound from behind him, and then it was only the small crisp *crunch!* of a snail shell and a tiny gasp of dismay. Will felt behind him, found an arm, and then down it to a woollen hand. They were only a dozen steps away from the shrubbery now, and from there their way was hidden.

Will knelt up cautiously, trying to push his eyes to the top of his head. Rosie had taken off her white cap, and all he could sense of her was warmth, and an alert solidness, and something else that was indefinable except as Rosie. He could see no sentries: nothing but darkness and chilly mist. The other guard must be right under the archway. Will got to his feet and Rosie got up with him.

She could not be so quiet once they were amongst the bushes; her skirts kept catching on branches and she had to be careful to avoid ripping the material. After a while she stopped and did something complicated to her skirts that seemed to make things easier. Will tried not to think much about it.

The world seemed to be waiting, absolutely quietly, as the mist settled over it into a veil. It seemed to take a long time until, drenched to the knees with ice-cold dew, they stole out of the shrubbery, climbed cautiously over the fence, and onto the rough verge of the drive. From there, the house could only be seen as a patch of particularly dense darkness against the charcoal of the hazy sky.

Everything was still, so still, as if the world had stopped. Every small sound echoed widely and then fled far, far into the emptiness around them.

'You'd better go straight away,' said Will, wishing he could merge with the air, grow, spread as the mist did, so that he could go with her, ahead of her, round her.

'Yes. Yes. Now I am here I must go. Will! Look after Sam for me, won't you.'

They were both talking quietly, rapidly, with their breath warm on each other's cheeks.

'I shall make a sign so you can tell it is safe to return,' said Will. 'I'll . . . I'll drive a cross of nails into the fence-post at the end of the drive.'

'Yes. And I shall come back as soon as I can. Will! Will, I shall always—'

And then a light flashed somewhere on the edge of Will's vision.

Chapter 33

Will snapped round his head, but it was too late. The light that had sprung into being from the direction of the outside world had widened too and swept up the drive and towards them. A huge inky shadow was springing away from Will's feet, such a monstrous, visible thing that he actually jumped back, as if to escape it. He pulled Rosie back out of the light. Then he turned hastily, tripped over three separate things, stumbled into the fence, and found he was holding Rosie's hand.

They were out of the light, now, most of the time, though the gauzy yellowness was jerking and swaying wildly as the man holding the lantern ran towards them, and sometimes the light would lick at Will's coat or glance over Rosie's sleeve. In a moment the man with the lantern would see them for certain. Will scooped Rosie up in a desperate rush and planted her on the top rail of the fence. Then he vaulted over himself, and had lifted her down and into the blessed shelter of the bushes before he'd even noticed how warm her body was under his hands.

There was a shout from the man with the lantern. It was answered from the house.

'What shall we do?' gasped Rosie.

'Quiet, quiet,' breathed Will, his face turned away from the drive in case the light should catch it, and holding her head down against his shoulder.

But then there was another shout, and then another. Rosie went to get up, but Will tightened his grip on her. She was no match for his strength.

'*Listen*,' he breathed.

There were voices. It was impossible to hear the words, Will had to strain even to distinguish the tone of their speech. Will knelt on the frosty grass, staggered anew at his own stupidity: George had placed sentries at the far end of the drive, as well as round the house. But of course he would have done. Will had only thought about the sentries' being there to stop people escaping; but of course, of course, they were chiefly to warn of people coming from outside.

How could I forget there is a war all round us? he thought. Why am I such a fool, a fool, a fool?

There were echoing footsteps, now, running towards them: a group of men. Will buried his face in Rosie's scented hair.

The footsteps clattered nearer, drew level, and stopped for several heart-pounding seconds. Then they started off again into the blackness. Will relaxed enough to breathe.

'They think they saw something,' he said, in the smallest possible whisper, 'but they aren't sure what it was.'

And now, from the house, was another group of men, their lanterns shining clear and yellow and wide.

And then a sharp challenge.

'Who goes there?'

George. That was George's voice. Will's sleeve twitched as Rosie's fingers tightened on it.

'Friend.'

The two groups met only half a dozen feet away. Will's leg was cramping and he had to shift himself to ease it. He did it gently, gently, as faces appeared, pale and flat in the light of the lanterns. They flickered in the black air, disembodied, like gargoyles, but full of force.

Will put his hand forward onto the mud to remind himself of the realness of everything: even the warmth of a sigh might reach those cold faces and give them away. He wanted to warn Rosie, but he didn't dare.

'What's going on?' asked George's voice: and it came from one of the gargoyles. Will blinked hard, and looked again and saw that the gargoyle and George were the same: it was his friend, Mr Gilfry's son, the brave young hero of the war. But a gargoyle, too, carved by the light.

'We thought we saw someone, Corporal.'

'Thought?'

'We're pretty sure, Corporal.'

'A King's man?'

'We only saw a bit of a shadow, Corporal. But maybe.'

The faces were coming together until they formed a golden ring like a fantastic crown.

'Well, in that case we must find him, if he's to be found. We don't want him running back with news of our hotel, do we, lads?'

A smear of greyness from one of the lanterns licked along the top of the fence as the men moved. It just touched the edge of Rosie's shoulder, though no one but Will saw it.

George was giving instructions to his men. They were going to separate and search every inch within a couple of hundred yards.

But if they did that, they would find Rosie: they would take her away, and she would belong to George for ever. And Will would not be able to bear it.

The men were moving off with a tramping of boots and a clinking of muskets and buckles. Will carefully shifted himself away from Rosie a little, took hold of her round arms.

'Stay still,' he whispered. 'I shall show myself, and draw the men towards the house after me. Wait until they are past you, and then you will be able to get away.'

'But Will—'

But the men were dispersing and Will had to move at once, while the noise gave him some cover.

'Stay safe, Rosie,' he whispered; and moved. He ran bent double through the bushes. When he got to the edge of the rough grassland which had once been the lawn he stopped. There were lanterns bobbing in every direction like marsh-ghosts. He reached down and dug his fingers into the clammy soil and found a stone.

He threw it hard. It rose over the still land, stretching an invisible arc in the charcoal sky, and landed with a *snick!* somewhere. The lanterns swung sharply, and waited.

Another stone. This one was heavier, and so it carried further. It tacked and bounced and tacked twice more, unmistakably.

Someone shouted.

Will took his deepest breath and launched himself out of the striped shadows of the bushes. It would take him several long seconds to get to the next bit of shelter, but in that time a man could hardly—

The shots must have missed him by yards, but he leapt like a hare as he ran. Behind him men were shouting and cursing, and everything was in confusion. The grass was striped with long shadows from the trees, but Will felt as though he was outlined in light, as if he were burning, flickering, drawing fire.

Will lunged into a long strip of shadow and his foot caught something hard—a low plinth that had perhaps once held some statue—and he went flying. He hit the ground full-length, grunted, slid, and lay still.

'Here! There was something here, Corporal!'

The darkness swallowed the words hungrily.

'Can you see it now?'

Will gasped at the empty air. He moved a little, groaned almost silently, pushed himself painfully to his knees, and then, after a swaying pause, to his feet.

He was lucky: he'd fallen along an inky stretch which streamed from the base of a broad holly tree.

'Not just now, Corporal. But he can't be far.'

The shadows shifted as the men held their lanterns higher. And then the moon, the hunters' moon, slid quietly through the clouds. It hung above them, glistening and treacherous, and the world spread itself out around them, wider than Will had thought the world could be.

And a deer, black as soot, took fright at its own shadow and ran, crashing invisibly through the undergrowth.

One of George Gilfry's men moved, and there was an explosion that left Will's ears ringing.

'There!' someone called. 'There, Corporal! D'you hear him?'

'There!' called someone further away. 'See the bushes move?'

'Quick!' bellowed George. 'After him, lads! A silver shilling to the man who brings him down!'

Will stood, heart pounding, in the slick of the concealing shadow, while the moon hung above the empty country as bright and sharp as a blade. He waited and watched as the sounds of the men grew distant, until they faded away. He listened hard, his senses as tight as a mouse's: but he could hear nothing behind him on the drive—no cautious footstep or rustle of skirts.

She was gone, then.

Will stood, looking towards the outside world after her, feeling suddenly as hollow as the shell of the sky.

But then something happened in the hugeness of that outside world. There was a ruffle, like the passage of a breeze.

But there was no breeze.

It disturbed the cobalt beauty of the land. Will stared, blinked hard, and rubbed his eyes. There was . . . something. Something not sharp, like the trees that rose above the settling mist, but fuzzy-edged. And there was . . . not quite a sound, but a low vibration that trembled the air very slightly.

Like horses. Horses a long way away.

Yes, horses, that was what it was, a long line of them, some of them in pairs, but most of them trotting raggedly as they picked their way along the dark road. And there, yes, there were their riders: men in tall hats, with white on their tunics that occasionally flashed through the gloom.

King's men.

King's men, who had been alerted by those shots and were even now turning into the far-away end of the drive.

There were a few long moments when Will hesitated, unable to pull his mind completely free of that small area of the huge tumbling world which was filled with Rosie.

But she was gone, was gone, was gone. And George and his men were gone, too, chasing the echo of some silly deer.

And here were King's men coming. Lots of them.

Will turned away from all of them and ran full tilt back towards the house.

Chapter 34

Will pelted thumpingly down the drive, through the clattering archway, and across to the faint light that spilled under the kitchen door.

The kitchen was full of sleeping people, for just about every bed in the house had been claimed by the soldiers. Will looked round hastily in the light of the dying fire. Sam was curled, as quiet as a baby, on the mat; Toby had his head down on the table; and Mrs Keen was snoring in the chair by the grate.

'Wake up!' shouted Will, and he banged hard on the table with his fist. 'There are more soldiers coming. Quick, wake up!' Toby came awake with a start and a grunt and only saved himself from falling because his head crashed into a chair-back.

Mrs Keen snorted into wakefulness. She blinked through the gloom, gathering her shawl protectively round her great bulk.

'Will?' she asked, a little querulous. 'What is it? Will?'

'We must get away from here,' Will said. 'All of us. Up to the tower, I think. There are King's men coming, and there's sure to be fighting. We can lock ourselves in and no one will know we are there.'

Toby rubbed his head with a thick-fingered hand.

'You could have made me crack my head open,' he grumbled, still half asleep.

'I'm sorry, but come on, now, come on! We must rouse Mr Gilfry.'

Mr Gilfry was awake already. The master was awake, too, squeezed back as far as he could into his corner. As soon as the master saw Will he put the kaleidoscope up to his eye, turning the tube so that the tiny pieces of glass tumbled from mirror to mirror like minuscule icicles.

'What's happening?' asked Mr Gilfry. 'I heard some shots a little while ago.'

'There's a troop of horsemen at the end of the drive. They must have seen the muzzle-flashes of those shots, even if they didn't hear them. They'll be coming to see what's what.'

Mr Gilfry sat up, and winced as his leg shot pain through him yet again.

'Who are they, Will? King's men or rebels?'

The moon had leached every tiny bit of colour out of the world, but Will had seen enough.

And Mr Gilfry, stuck in this narrow room, had seen nothing.

'Mr Gilfry, I'm sorry, I truly am. But . . . but they're the enemy.'

Will found himself on the end of a straight gaze. Then Mr Gilfry looked away.

'This is bad news for George,' he said, quietly.

'George is a fine soldier, with men to do his command,' said Will. 'And we are best out of his way. We shall go up to the tower and then, if there is any fighting, we shall not get caught in the middle of it. Here, Mr Gilfry. I shall lay the stretcher on the bed, and then that will be easy for both of us.'

'You would make a fine nursemaid,' muttered Mr Gilfry, with some bitterness, manoeuvring himself painfully onto the tarred canvas.

Mrs Keen came in, her shadow near as wide as the door.

'Will, you take care of the master,' she said. 'Toby and I shall manage the stretcher, and then I shall run along to the mistress. She'll certainly come out when she hears this news, if I can only make her listen. Oh, but my hands are tender sore. Toby, have you got hold of those poles? Then one-two-three lift!'

Will helped them negotiate the turn of the door.

'Take me out of the kitchen door and across the yard,' ordered Mr Gilfry. 'That's the straightest way.'

'No, don't,' said Will. 'Take the back stairs. It'll be awkward, but you must not be out in the yard when the troopers come.'

Mr Gilfry rolled a baleful eye at him, but Will was already turning to the little man in the corner who was turning, turning the tube of the kaleidoscope uselessly in the dark.

'Master,' said Will, speaking softly and damping down his impatience as well as he could. 'We are going up to the tower, now. Do you remember? Where all your books are.'

But the master turned the kaleidoscope round and round in dry fingers and gave no sign of hearing. Will put a hand on his arm, but the sinews stiffened under his fingers, rigid as wood.

'I won't take it from you,' said Will, as carefully gentle as he could be, with the clock ticking and the war rushing closer. 'Don't you remember, it was me that helped you make it? I took the colours out of the window, and cut the pieces of mirror to shape. And then we put them together in the tube.'

But the man was far away, out of reach, searching fruitlessly for patterns in the dark kaleidoscope. Will was torn between his huge haste and a dreadful pity.

'All right,' he said, resolutely. 'Well, I'm not leaving you here to be pulled about and killed by that lot that are coming—or those that are already here—so you must come with me. And as you won't let go of the kaleidoscope I can't take you on my back. So you must walk. Come, then. Up you get. You can still look into the kaleidoscope, if you like, but walk you must.'

Will hauled him up, but the man's legs stayed bent and stiff, even when Will shook him a little. Will couldn't hold him for more than a second or two. He put the man back down more or less gently and wondered what on earth he could do.

Someone came to the doorway behind him, and nearly all the small chinks of moonlight that had bounced and skidded in from the outside world were blotted out.

'Will,' said Sam's clear voice. 'I've brought the bath chair.'

Will was ready almost to weep with gratitude.

'I could not have managed on my own, Sam,' he said.

Sam set his mouth in a determined line.

'You do not have to manage on your own,' he said. 'Not while I'm around, Will. Never.'

Will could not have managed on his own. He spared Sam as much as he could, but he would have near broken his back heaving the master up the stairs without him.

'Help me get him past the tapestry and onto the tower stairs,' said Will, 'and then he'll be safe.'

Sam's eyes glittered at him through the darkness.

'Rosie isn't safe, though, is she,' he said. 'She's gone. Gone right away. I know she has, because she told me to help you, and to do what you said.'

Will paused for a moment to look out through the stone skeleton of the great window. Near the house there were gauzy spheres of light swinging along towards the black line of the courtyard wall. He could hear voices, too, men's voices, grumbling at being called out on a wild goose—a wild *deer*—chase. And far behind the voices there was perhaps the rumble of hooves on mud—though down on the ground, surrounded by voices and tramping feet, it might not be possible to hear it.

Where in all that great hemisphere of darkness was Rosie? She could not have got past the King's men. She must be out there, alone, in the dark . . .

'Rosie told me to look after you, too, Sam,' said Will, slowly. 'But I've done that, now, haven't I?'

'I'm all right,' said Sam. 'Anyway, I can look after myself. Mostly.'

Will took a new hold on the master's skinny body and found that his mind was made up. However the night spun, he would add his penny-weight to it.

'Let's see you and the master safe on the tower stairs,' he said. 'And then I had better go and find out what is happening.'

'Will you find Rosie?' asked Sam.

'Aye. If I can.'

Will ran down between the pinnacled shadows of the stairs. It was no good making a plan, even if he'd had the wits to work one out, for the world was turning fast, now: even keeping his feet on the ground would not be easy.

There was a burst of shouting and laughter from the courtyard. George's men had returned, and they were feeling safer for the false alarm, almost victorious. Will turned to the right, slipping through the doorway that led to the Great Hall.

There were candles burning on the long table—more candles than usually were lit in the whole house—but even so the walls vanished into darkness before they reached the huge timbers of the roof.

Will jogged swiftly through the flickering dimness. He was only just in time, for George's men were coming in the main door, eager to settle themselves down again. They were nipped with the cold and looking for more ale. Will ran down through the kitchen and opened the outside door a crack. Out in the chilly dark of the courtyard George was giving orders for the sentries to return to their beats, all unknowing that the world had moved on, on, catastrophically, while their eyes had been turned another way.

Will slipped out and round the corner to the kitchen garden.

Will faltered, then. He had come this far, but the task in front of him was as huge as the sky. How could he find Rosie? They were only two tiny fragments of humanity, and in front of him was all the perilous wide world.

But there was no good thinking about it, not with a brain like his. He must just blunder on, that was all, and hope—and if that was foolish, well, foolishness was what he was best at, after all.

He went to take a step forward; but as he did the darkness moved.

Will drew himself together, braced himself ready to duck, swerve, run.

But then the darkness spoke.

'Will?' it said, in a small, uncertain voice; and Will's anxiety melted.

'Here,' he said, opening his arms. 'Here I am.'

Rosie took a step towards him, and then another, and another, until she could come no closer.

'More soldiers,' she whispered. 'They're coming. A whole troop of them. King's men. They are on the drive, so I couldn't get past. I had to come back. Oh, Will, is there no escape from all this terrible war?'

Will held on to her. Surely she was right, and there was no escape: except that if the world could tumble Rosie into his arms then he would not give up hope of anything.

'Perhaps there might be,' he said. 'Come, Rosie. We shall hide you in the tower. The others are there.'

'But—'

'And then,' Will went on, grimly, 'the fighting men can fight all they please. Now, Rosie!'

Here, at last, I have come to the centre, the hub of all the world.
And everything is black.
Black, for death.

Chapter 35

The tower room was almost completely dark, but Will could feel that it was crowded. The master was sitting in his chair at his desk, and seemed more like a man than he had for some time.

'It seems to do him good being here, poor soul,' said Mrs Keen. 'He feels safer, perhaps.'

'May it be true,' said Mr Gilfry, his face as pale as chalk in a patch of moonlight. 'Sam! What can you see, there?'

Sam had his hands cupped round his eyes as he leaned against the glass of the little window.

'The men are still stopped,' he reported. 'At least, I can't see them, really, Mr Gilfry, but I think I would if they moved.'

'Stopped where?' asked Will. 'They're on the drive, aren't they?'

'Yes, but they're still up by the long field.'

Mr Gilfry grunted.

'The drive's badly overgrown just there: remember how the trees swept the sides of the wagon?'

'They'll think they're lost,' said Miss Winter. 'They'll decide they were mistaken about those shots. They'll think it was a poacher, or some accident, and go away.'

Toby let out something between a sigh and a groan.

'That's the end of us, then,' he said, quaveringly. 'George's men will stay here until the road's quieter, and then they'll cut all our throats and set the house afire and clear off. That's how it'll be. You see? Even being a coward's no protection in this wicked world.'

'Or being a woman, or a child,' said Mrs Keen, quietly.

Will went over to where the scruffy outline of Sam's head was visible against the deepest violet of the sky. He felt down the window frame to find the tinderbox on the sill and then he made his way back through the warm people to the master's desk. He climbed up onto it, searching with his hands for the place where the lamp was hooked onto the chain that came down from the ceiling.

The lamp was heavier than he'd thought. He had to be careful as he got down from the desk again not to spill the oil that slopped about inside it. He went back through the dark to the window, and Sam made way for him.

The striking of the flint sounded loud, and the room seemed to gasp as the spark jumped and flared and died.

'What are you doing?' asked Mr Gilfry, sharply. 'Will?'

But Will did not heed him. He struck at the flint

again, and this time the minute point of white grew to a glow that illuminated the tinderbox. Mr Gilfry was saying something, but Will was blowing gently on the glowing embers until they eased sideways and caught fire.

The wick of the lamp resisted the flame for a couple of seconds. Then it budded orange and blue, dipped, and flickered, and became a steady light.

The master made a noise like a moan and pointed the kaleidoscope into the centre of it. But Will turned away from him.

'Will,' said Mr Gilfry, 'Will, is there not some other way? Will, you might be bringing George to his death!'

'George is strong, Mr Gilfry, and a fighter,' said Will. 'And the rest of us must live.'

He was holding the lamp aloft, turning the tower into a swinging sphere of shadows, when what he had said hit him like a hammer-blow. 'Oh, I would have us all live if I could,' he cried, 'but I cannot turn the whole world. Tell me how I can, Mr Gilfry, and I will, even if it costs me my own life. I give you my word of it.'

Mr Gilfry took in a deep juddering breath.

'I thought I'd finished with war,' he said. 'For war snaps us up and turns us desperate cruel and there is nothing that can be done about it.'

Will held the lamp at the window for twenty long seconds, then moved it away for a space, and then put it back by the glass again. He did this half a dozen times, until someone said:

'I can hear them.'

And Will himself became aware, even through the glass, of the steady rumbling of hooves on the mud of the drive.

He snuffed out the flame between finger and thumb, and the room went black as hell. The tower window was perhaps a foot wide, and four feet high. All it showed was charcoal smudges of landscape under a sharp silver moon, and, underneath them, the black pit of the courtyard.

'Is the door at the bottom of the stairs bolted fast?' asked Miss Winter, into the waiting air.

Will nodded, then realized he couldn't be seen.

'Tight fast, ma'am.'

Sam's voice piped up:

'It's a very *thick* door, isn't it, Will?'

'Certainly it is,' answered Will, stoutly. 'Oak, that is, and hundreds of years old. Nearly as hard as iron: and the bolts and hinges *are* iron.'

'It's well hidden, too, behind the tapestry, Sam,' said Mrs Keen. 'No stranger would ever know we were here.'

'Come away from that window, Sam,' said Rosie.

'But I want to—'

'Never mind that. Once people start messing about with firearms you never know where the bullets might go.'

Will squeezed Sam's shoulder and gave him a small push in the direction of Rosie's voice.

There was the crack of a shot. Everybody jumped, even though it was too far away to be loud.

'What can you see, Will?' asked Rosie.

'Nothing,' said Will, shielding his eyes and pushing his nose against the glass.

'It is so dark,' said Miss Winter, very quietly. 'It's hard to believe that anything is stirring. Oh!'

'Another shot,' said Rosie. Will might have seen a faint reflected glow of the muzzle-flash, but he couldn't be sure.

'What is George doing?' muttered Mr Gilfry. 'Where are his sentries?'

'Dead,' said Toby, darkly. 'It stands to reason. Who else would those men be firing at?'

The rumbling of the hooves had ceased again, but now the horses were so close that Will could hear even the occasional restless stamp.

'They must be just outside the archway,' whispered Miss Winter. 'I believe—'

There was an order, a sharp order, and Miss Winter's next words were masked by the long growl of hooves under the archway.

There was a single shaft of moonlight that shone across the courtyard and bumpily over the cobbles into the door of the barn. And there, there, as the column bumped and clattered into the courtyard through it, was a flash of white—and another—and a third, just to be sure: slices of pipe-clayed cross-belts.

King's men.

And then there was another heart-thudding pause followed by the tack of a pair of feet hitting the cobbles.

Shh!

Will had said it even as Toby was opening his mouth. Toby started, and then hunched his head into his shoulders—two unmistakable movements, even charcoal on black—but there was no longer any need for quiet, for below them came a succession of echoing thuds, wood on wood, musket stock on the oak of the main door.

Someone somewhere in the tower let out a small cry.

'Will,' whispered Rosie, tremblingly, 'the front door is fast, isn't it?'

Will turned, and then couldn't see her.

'Yes,' he said, 'but not against—'

There was a huge head-reeling crash and the whole house shuddered violently. Dust swirled up round them in a storm of must.

'That's the lock gone,' observed Toby, with resignation, through the ringing in their ears. 'No iron could stand against a volley of musket balls at close range. They'll be into the house, now.'

Someone whimpered, and someone said *there, there,* and Will said *shh!* again.

'We have good hopes the soldiers will never guess we are here,' he said, steadily. 'They will have seen the light, but in the dark they'll not have been able to judge its height. We must be as quiet as—'

And then there was a great roar, as if the doors to eternity had burst open under them.

Will said something, but he couldn't hear what it was he'd said. So he said it again; but the noise from below was going on and on and on. A mortal man's breath would have given out, but the yell of heroes, of fighting men, went on and on, filling the house, awe-inspiring and impossible: sixty tongues bellowing a long war-cry of rage and fear and exhilaration.

Amidst the clamour were more musket shots, and a clanging like dropped saucepans, but all these sounds were puny amidst the shattering racket of bellowing men. Will found himself talking out loud to himself, though he hardly knew what he was saying.

It is a battle, he sort-of said, through lips that made no impression on the quivering air of the tower. *They are fighting against the enemy, full of honour and skill, spilling out their lifeblood for their cause.*

But his soundless words had no power to print themselves on the air, or in his brain.

Will had turned away from the window without knowing what he had done. And now some part of the darkness of the tower had grown solid, warm, and it was close against him. He clung to it with all the strength of a drowning man.

Chapter 36

At long last the dawn stole into the courtyard. The violet light yielded to the dullest grey, and then, like magic, there appeared on the dark cobbles below straggles of even greater darkness as silently, without any effort or human hand, the grey world flushed into inglorious brightness.

Rosie would not let Sam look; but most of the others came, and looked long and gravely at the rubbish in the yard. Even Toby was silenced by it.

'Is George there?' asked Mr Gilfry, at long last, imprisoned in his chair.

'No, Mr Gilfry. Not that we can tell,' said Will.

Mrs Keen shook her head.

'But other men's sons,' she said, soberly.

Sam looked up at Rosie.

'Are they dead?' he asked.

Rosie pushed back his hair from his pale face.

'It's hard to be sure from here, Sam. But I'm afraid they are dead, yes.'

Sam frowned, and kicked back at the wall with his feet.

'The horses will need watering,' he said. 'The

trough in the top field leaks a bit. I have to top it up every day.'

'You're a good boy, but we must all stay quietly here, Sam, for now. They will have to wait.'

Soon there was movement down in the courtyard. Men and horses walked below them in an endlessly changing pattern of red and white and black and chestnut and grey. Will stood a little way back from the window and watched it; and he understood why the master kept his eye to the little tumbling tube of the kaleidoscope.

'I hope they dispose of—of *them*, properly,' said Toby, gruffly, with a jerk of his head towards the window. 'Six feet under they have to be, or they'll be poisoning the land. And they'd better keep 'em well clear of the well, too, or there'll be plague about, you mark my words.'

A man was being led out into the yard. His hair was dark as ebony. He wasn't George. He strolled quietly, looking out through the archway at the trees, black above their crimson and gold carpet, and at the silver sky. But he was led to the wall beside it.

Eight men stood in a row in front of him, like a game of grandmother's footsteps, like pawns: red pawns, and their heads were solid wood.

The orders came up to them through the thin glass: one, two, three shouts. And then there was a crash of almost-together muskets.

When Will opened his eyes he was watching the changing patterns of the courtyard kaleidoscope

244

again; and he wished the colours had no more meaning than that of the tumbling glass.

'Will,' said Mr Gilfry, hoarsely, 'was that—'

'No' said Will. 'No, it was someone else.'

Mr Gilfry drew in a long loud breath.

'Keep watch, lad, and tell me if you see him,' he said.

'We cannot stay here for ever,' said Mrs Keen, shifting uncomfortably, some hours later.

'But we cannot leave the tower,' said Miss Winter.

'No,' said Toby. 'Course we can't. We couldn't think of it. Those men, they're savages, brutal.'

'We shall die of thirst, if we stay here,' said Rosie.

Mr Gilfry grunted.

'They've stopped digging, by the sound of it.'

Toby shook his head.

'I hope they've not put them in the kitchen garden. There were some promising sprouts, I had, there.'

'They will have other things to do,' said Will. 'They will go in the end.'

The kaleidoscope twisted and chinked in the master's dry fingers.

'Red, orange, yellow,' he muttered. 'Yes, yes. A fire would purify everything. There. There. Good.'

The air in the tower room went solid with fear.

* * *

'What's that?'

Will turned away from the window for the first time in a hour. The scarlet men below were leading out their horses, cream and strawberry and bay.

There was a faint scratching coming from somewhere above their heads.

'It sounds like a bird,' said Sam, uncertainly.

'I think you're right, Sam,' said Rosie. 'There must be pigeons up in the roof.'

Miss Winter frowned.

'I have never known there to be birds in the roof before.'

They listened.

'It sounds more like a cat,' said Mrs Keen, and now she was whispering. 'I think it is too stealthy a noise for a bird.'

Toby tipped back his head on his thick neck.

'Where's that trapdoor lead to?' he asked.

Miss Winter stared upwards.

'There cannot be any part of this house I have not explored,' she said, slowly. 'My brother had a passion for small places, and darkness, as a boy. Why, *finding* him was often a challenge, indeed. But I do not remember . . . '

'There's a spur that comes off the main house, ma'am,' said Mr Gilfry. 'The roof of this tower joins it. It may be—'

They all froze. Someone or something had found the trapdoor. Someone—it must be some*one*—was trying to undo the catch, but it was stuck. He was struggling with it, up there in the dimness where the grey daylight shouldered its way between the old slates.

'Come back to the walls,' said Will, suddenly. 'He might—'

There was a crash as the catch came free. The hatch door swung down on its hinges, banged against the frame, and came to a stop. Decades of dust swirled out of the opening to pepper the master's black coat.

Then the soles of two shoes appeared, and a length of thin shanks, and two hands, clutching whitely at the frame of the door.

And then, like some gargoyle, they saw a face.

It was George's.

Chapter 37

George's face was twisted into a grimace like an old man's. He launched himself down from the trapdoor and landed with hardly a stagger on the master's desk, smashing the satinwood letter-stand to ruin with one heavy heel. He was grinning, teeth bared, like a cornered dog.

'George,' said Mr Gilfry, steadily, behind him; and George started round.

Two pairs of blue eyes found each other.

'Welcome home, George,' said Mr Gilfry, with a smile.

George jumped down from the desk. Will winced at the noise his heels made on the floor. Any sound might be heard down below, even though most of the soldiers were out in the courtyard, now, or under the black earth.

'I knew you would be here,' said George, almost snarling. 'Hiding.'

There was a moment's silence. Then Mr Gilfry said:

'We here are not made to be fighters, George.'

George swept his arm round in a furious gesture and cleared half the master's desk. Rosie was just in time to prevent a heavy book thudding to the floor.

'Not made to be fighters?' he demanded. 'You're fit to die, aren't you? Because that's all it needs.' He stood, blinking and swaying a little, as if the room was whirling round him. Then he went on, taking great short gasps as if the air itself was not to be trusted. 'Have you any idea, any idea at all, what's been going on beneath your feet? Twenty men, I had. Twenty. The best band of men you'd find in the whole army. My companions, they were. My brothers. Men who'd come with me wherever I led them. And do you know what? They are all dead, now, save me. I led them here and they were trapped. And then all they could do was to sell themselves as dearly as they might, because two deaths must be a better bargain than one.'

The tiny fragments of glass tumbled in their tube.

'I'm truly sorry,' said Mr Gilfry, quietly. 'And I'm truly proud that you have been so much respected amongst your fellows, George.'

But this only sparked greater, wilder anger in his son.

'But they are *gone*!' he said, far too loudly, for under their feet were soldiers, soldiers, with pistol and musket and bayonet and sword, all ready and hungry for use.

Who wins a war?

The strongest: that's all that counts.

Will took a step forward, but George wheeled

249

round and suddenly there was a knife in his friend's hand. Its shining blade, skilfully sharpened, was only a couple of feet from Will's heart.

'They were betrayed,' George said, staring at Will along the gleaming blade. 'They must have been, to bring a troop of King's men here in the middle of the night. The poor fools were betrayed.'

'It was my doing,' said the master, matter-of-factly. 'I did not want you, or your kind, here. You are a disturbance. Untrustworthy. Having you killed was the most effective way. Most *satisfactory* way.'

George slashed the knife round in a great arc and everyone jumped back from it.

'You old fool,' he almost shouted. 'You've destroyed everything. They've killed them all and . . . ' For a moment he seemed on the verge of tears, but then he slashed viciously at the air again with his knife and got himself back under control.

'George,' said Rosie, quietly, 'listen to me. You do not understand—'

'Oh, I understand!' He turned to her, almost pleading with her. 'Can't you see the injustice of it all? Even now? Look at him! The master. Why, he is not even master of his own wits. And look at his sister! What good has she ever done? Has anyone ever loved her? What right has *she* to be alive?'

He took two sudden steps across the room and seized Miss Winter's arm: and all in a second she had stumbled forward and been turned by a strong hand, and he was holding her against him, like a shield; and the gleaming knife was floating beside her pale throat.

There was a frozen moment while George's eyes glared round at them all.

'What right has *she* to breathe?' he demanded. 'Why should I not slit her throat when my friends, my comrades, brave men, fine men, all lie dead? Why should she live uselessly while the best part of us are finished?'

'George,' began Mrs Keen, but Will took a step forward.

'Because she has done no harm,' he said. 'We call her mistress, but she has no say over what happens. And the master, too: his head is filled with dreams. I am more to blame than either of them.'

'You?' said George, staring, startled, white as plaster.

'Yes,' said Will. 'For it wasn't Miss Winter who made sure the King's men came here and found you. It was me.'

Chapter 38

'Will!' cried Rosie, and her voice split the silence of the tower room like a wedge through wood. 'Oh, Will, you fool, you fool!'

'I signalled to the King's men,' said Will, not taking his eyes from George's for a moment. 'They were on the point of turning away, you see, and I wanted them to come.'

George was gazing at him in amazement, and the knife he was holding at Miss Winter's white throat wavered.

'But why you?' he said. 'You are nothing, Will. Why should you help them?'

'To save Rosie, partly,' said Will. 'To save her from you and your men. And also in the hope you would all fight each other and go away. Because if I could get rid of every fighting man in the country, I would. You have heads solid through, each of you, killing and burning and raping, and doing the bidding of someone so far away you cannot understand it.'

George was as pale as death, and his chest was heaving in long, unsteady breaths.

'*You?*' he breathed. 'You, the little nobody, are the cause of all this? Of all *this*?'

'George,' said Mr Gilfry, with sudden authority, 'George, you are not yourself at this moment. No one in your place could be. I understand what this has meant to you, and I respect it. But—'

'Hold your tongue!' screamed George, and shoved Miss Winter away so that she stumbled and fell at Mr Gilfry's feet.

Mr Gilfry reached out a rough hand and pulled her up and out of the way.

'George,' said Rosie, 'stop, I beg you. It was the only thing Will could do. He did not do it lightly.'

But George, unheeding, walked forward two steps and slashed the knife at Will's face in a vicious whizz of steel.

Will threw himself backwards, and crashed into a bookcase. He ducked sideways, but the tip of the knife caught him. It skidded lopsidedly through the skin of his forehead, off his skull, and away.

Will went down into a crouch. The knife was above him, ready to stab, so he threw himself forwards into George's legs, and George folded and went over the top of him. There was a graunching of moving furniture and the clattering of a falling chair, but Will, with the knife somewhere behind him, was too busy turning and scrambling up to think about it.

The knife was jutting accusingly from George's hand. George hissed, changed his grip, and lunged. Will tried to get away, but the master's desk was behind him and he overbalanced backwards onto it with his belly exposed and his feet kicking round urgently.

And then suddenly the knife was above him, and so was George's face, ugly with hatred, and all Will could do was to lash out blindly.

One foot kicked emptiness, but the other made contact with something. The face above him grunted and creased and receded for a second so Will kicked out again, but he was nearly as useless as a beetle on its back.

And here was the knife above him again, and any moment now—

Will's hand closed on something beside him on the desk, and he hit out with it as hard as he could. It struck George's descending arm and exploded in a fountain, a deluge, of black.

The knife went off course and thumped into the leather of the desk. Will rolled sideways, and then he was falling, swift and hard. He hit the ground, rolled some more, and managed to find space to get up. George was wiping his sleeve across his eyes, blinking and cursing, and his face was a splatter of pink and grey and speckled black. But then all the colours of the world seemed to have gone mad, for Will's own hand was red, bright red.

Red and black, red and black, like the chessmen, with heads of solid wood or ivory.

A thought went through Will's head like a bullet: *I am a fighting man.*

And he jettisoned all other thought and gave himself up to the kill.

There was a singing joy in this: a delight in having one aim, one clear motive, one huge need and strong purpose. There was pleasure in using all his strength, which was so new to him, not carefully, steadily, cautiously, but in a massive explosion of power. He was no longer fighting George: he was no longer fighting a person, even; he was just fighting—swinging and hitting, and yet calculating, too. Assessing the reach of the knife, the speed of it; watching the other calculating brain behind it; and everything was happening in a series of flashing instants as he lunged and ducked and tumbled on the edge of blood and death. The world was falling around him, breaking; people were crying out and squashing themselves away: but none of it was happening in his world, where everything was simple and absorbing and glorious.

The enemy had lost its knife, so they were even, now. Its breath was labouring, harsh, heavy. It was getting minutely slower—though the mind behind the grey mask was chisel-sharp. Will aimed a blow, found it dodged, and then the enemy's teeth had closed like a vice on his wrist. Will tried once, twice, with huge grunting efforts, to shake the thing off, but it wouldn't come; and so he raised his other arm high and chopped it down with all his strength on the enemy's neck.

That loosened it, at last—knocked it down onto the floor—had its nose in the dust. Will threw himself down onto it, sat on it, closed his hands round its neck and squeezed and tugged with all the strength in his craftsman's fingers.

But the enemy was strong, too, and it was

bucking and turning and squirming, and suddenly Will was off-balance, toppling sideways; and the enemy's knee was jerking up brutally at his groin.

And now Will was bellowing and curling up with the shock of the whiting pain, curling protectively around himself, but still aware that he was exposing his head, his neck, his back, the soles of his feet, to the murderous enemy.

And now the enemy was on him and there was nothing he could do: not with the pain roaring round him and all his strength dissolved into juddering gouts of deepening red.

This was the end of it, then. But that was the nature of fighting, that the weaker side lost. It was the justice of the world, the order of things, from the mighty spinning globe right down to the spider and the fly.

Will accepted it.

He waited for the pain to stop.

Chapter 39

The enemy fell on Will's spine in a solid grunting mass.

And then everything seemed to stop.

Will felt the impact only a little, because there were so many pains all round him, all screaming and clamouring for his attention. But still, there was something final about the way the enemy stilled for that one moment, and then slid unresisting to the floor.

The silence in the room was as sudden and as deep as a cliff.

Will tried to open his eyes, but only one of them was working. He squinted down at the wooden floor as he heaved in lungful after lungful of ancient dust. The wood was all a splatter of red and brown and black.

A thought came into his head from far far away: *that'll take a power of sanding*, he thought.

Now someone's hands were touching him. Words were being spoken, questions: quietly at first, and then urgently. But they were too small and distant for him to hear or bother about. Will waited until all his weight had settled back into its right place, and his mind had carefully withdrawn into a pattern that he recognized as his own; and then he tried to lift his head.

He was being hoisted up; he didn't know by whom, or where they wanted him to go, but he was too bewildered to think of resisting. He pushed down with his feet and felt the floor under them—but found that the world was pitching too crazily for him to stand. He was being half led, half carried, to a thing that seemed made to sit upon. So he sat, and discovered that he was dizzy and ready to faint through lack of breath. He breathed and breathed.

Someone had hold of one of his hands. Someone was wiping at it with a cloth that shuddered stickily across his skin, stinging sharp as a wasp.

And now someone had a hand under his chin, lifting it. But he was too disorientated to hold his head up straight, and everything overturned giddily until the white ceiling was glaring down at him.

A face came into the whiteness. Beautiful, it was, that face, with dark eyes you could rest in. The lips were moving, saying something.

Someone was wiping his forehead. He would have flinched away, except that it would have meant turning away from the eyes, from the curl of dark hair that clung so roundly to the creamy skin.

He found himself trying to smile at it, though smiling was painful, too. It was so unlike himself, that face, so far away from what he was; though in some strange way it felt part of him.

And he was safe, and at the end of things.

* * *

'Will?'

That word marked the instant, later, when the world took back its hold of him.

There was no use ignoring it, though he tried. It sucked him up and he had to go with it.

Will lowered his head from where it had been leaning back against a bookshelf and winced at the horrible crick in his neck. He raised an unsteady hand to rub at the pain.

He found himself staring at a small fearful face. Will opened his mouth to speak—and found he could make no noise at all.

'I brought you a drink, Will.'

Something was pushed against his lips. Will sipped, swilled the sweet water round his mouth, sipped again, and this time got enough to swallow. The water went down his sore throat like a brick, but he was thirsty, thirsty, thirsty for more and Will's hand had taken the cup and he was drinking, drinking, tipping up the tankard and shaking the last drops into his mouth.

He lowered the tankard at last.

'Thank you,' he said. 'Thank you, Sam.'

He thought of getting to his feet, and then decided to leave it for a time, for the world was still swaying under his feet and likely to tip him over. He opened his mouth to ask questions and found he didn't know how to begin.

'Mr Gilfry said I was to help you to come down,

Will, when you felt well enough,' said Sam.

Will leaned forward and gripped the arms of his chair. One of his hands was smarting, and his whole body seemed in need of a power of greasing.

'Could you give me a hand, please, Sam?' he asked. Sam picked up Will's arm and ducked his fair head underneath it.

'Course I can,' he said.

Chapter 40

The corpse was laid out on the table in the Great Hall. The bronze sheen of the polished oak reflected its hands and face dimly, as if its ghost were trapped there. Will stood between Mr Gilfry and Miss Winter and the horror of it shuddered the breath in his throat.

'I'm sorry,' he said.

''Twasn't your fault,' said Mr Gilfry, quietly. 'Never think that, Will. No, he was a fighter. That was his joy and his life. He was never going to come back to being a carpenter. And after all, 'twas only luck that I ever had him with me at all.'

Some memory sparked inside Will at that. Something else Mr Gilfry had once said about George. *I could never watch a boy grow up*, he had said, *and not feel as a father does to him*.

And this time Will understood what Mr Gilfry had been trying to say. And he realized, with a huge stab of grief, that he had lost a brother.

'I didn't know he'd died,' he said, at last. 'I don't remember . . . '

'My brother killed him,' said Miss Winter, quite white and still and passionless. 'George snatched the kaleidoscope from him—it was the nearest weapon to hand—and my brother went into a frenzy. Rosie had caught up George's knife out of the way, but none of us had thought about the penknife on the desk. All the anger my brother felt—the terror, I suppose, of the world's coming upon him—it burst out of him in an instant, and George died.' She took a quick deep breath. 'My brother was right, though,' she said. 'He was right to fear the world, and to hide from it. It was all any of us could do in the end.'

Mr Gilfry nodded quietly.

'Perhaps, ma'am. It is all too much for us, sometimes, true enough: but still we generally carry on long enough to pass on the fight to others.'

Will found his eyes horribly drawn to the yellow skin of the neck that rose so strongly from the collar of the green uniform. The wound was only a couple of inches long. It didn't seem anything like enough to have extinguished all the life in George Gilfry. Will found his muscles tensing, expecting George to come to life, full of anger and spirit and strength.

But the life was not there. Will could almost feel the lonely cold of the body that lay quietly on the great table which had itself seen generations of death and hope and death again.

'And the master?' he asked. 'Where is he?'

'Safe,' said Miss Winter. 'Back in his own world, where he is the master, and the world tumbles according to his needs.'

She seemed calmer than Will had ever known her.

'You know, he has struck out at me many times,' she went on, 'but I have never thought to hit him back. I had to, this time, for he was lashing out as if he was fighting the whole world, even the air, and the knife was in his hand. He swung it as if to stab me, and I struck his arm away before I knew what I was doing. And at that he gave up. He curled up and whimpered and sobbed. And I had won: won a fight against my brother.'

She laughed a short, wild laugh.

'Just think, all those years wasted on him, when all the time I could have fought my way free.'

'Miss Winter,' began Will; and then did not have words for what he wanted to say. But she turned swiftly to him.

'Do not be sorry for me,' she said. 'Not any more. For I have begun to make my own world at last.'

Will did not want to go to bed that night. He sat by the fire in the kitchen, gazing at the redness of the settling embers, too tired, too empty, to move or think or even sleep.

And then at last someone opened the door behind him.

He knew who it was without having to turn round.

She breathed warmth into his hair.

'Who are you?' she whispered.

It was an effort to come awake enough to answer.

'You know that, Rosie.'

She ran her hands along his shoulders and nuzzled a little at his hair as she shook her head.

'I thought I did. I thought you were Will the fool, Will nobody.'

Will smiled just a little.

'That sounds like me,' he said; but her hands were sliding down his sleeves to his own hands that were lying exhausted on the arms of the wooden chair. And now her breasts were behind him so that he felt himself sinking into them. Will moved his head just a little against the blissful warmth and softness behind him.

'So why should I have anything to do with you, Will Nunn?' she asked. 'I've always been decided I would find someone with a position, with a little money, who could keep me secure from want. That's only sensible. And you are nobody, Will, and you have nothing.'

'That's true, Rosie.'

'Then why am I here with you?'

He was too tired, too sleepy, to think; though, being so tired, the visions that floated into his view were very clear.

'We cannot understand it,' he said. 'It is all too big to see plainly.'

'But I have always been proud of my understanding, Will.'

'Yes. You have a good sharp brain, Rosie. Perhaps I'm good for a grindstone, I don't know. But still, there are things you cannot see straight. No one could. So much sanity would drive anyone mad.'

'And so we are all mad together, Will.'

'Yes,' he said, peacefully, gazing into the bright flames of the fire.

The sawyers had left the village years ago, off to seek adventure, or at least less dusty and thirsty work. Weeds had begun to struggle through the buttery dust in the saw pit.

'A week, it takes, in any case, to saw the elm planks for a coffin,' said Mr Gilfry. 'Even if we had the skill, and a seasoned tree to hand, we could not do it, Will.'

But Miss Winter had a key that opened an oak door that stood down half a flight of steps from the courtyard. Behind it were stacks of cold coffins, dusty with the webs of long-starved spiders. Will and Toby and Mrs Keen and Miss Winter struggled to lift them aside, and in the end they came to one two centuries old.

'This one'll be glad of some company, maybe,' said Toby, wiping the cold sweat off his brow.

Will broke the lock off easily, though he could not prevent the thin lead buckling a little.

Inside were only bits of bones, and dust, and something that gave out a minute flash of gold.

'A ring,' said Mrs Keen, a little tearful.

'It has outlasted even his bones,' said Miss Winter, marvelling. 'But still, we shall leave it where it is.'

They put George's body in on top of it.

'May they rest peacefully together,' said Mrs Keen, smoothing down his hair.

They stacked the coffins back as nearly as possible as they had found them, trying not to breathe in the dust that billowed round them, and climbed blinking back into the dull autumn day.

Mr Gilfry was waiting in his chair at the top of the steps.

'Is it all done?' he asked, and the sadness in his eyes echoed something inside Will. It reflected it, perhaps, like a mirror; doubled it; made it into a pattern, as if even their grief might in the end make some sort of sense.

'All done, Mr Gilfry,' he said.

'George has his wish, then,' said Mr Gilfry. 'He has ended a great man, equal with the family. That will allow him to rest easy, maybe.'

'Nothing can harm him now,' said Mrs Keen.

Chapter 41

Will and Toby and Sam brought the wagon back through one long anxious night. Once it was home they attacked the trees alongside the drive with billhook and axe, and dragged branches through the mud to cover up any signs that anything had ever come that way. They even made a barricade that might possibly be taken to be part of the rest of the hedge. There had been proclamations of a great victory, but that meant there would be bands of men about the country making their way home, if they had any homes left to go to.

The weather had turned vicious, hurling icy winds at the house and depositing pearls of hail on the dark staircase.

'You must board up the window, Will,' said Miss Winter, slipping and nearly falling head-first.

Will scratched his head.

'I think we could put the glass back, ma'am,' he suggested. 'There's not much missing, and we could fill that in with bottle glass, perhaps.'

But Miss Winter would not have it.

'A light might shine through and be seen,' she said. And she had the tower window boarded up, too. It meant that the master had always to have a lamp burning, but he seemed content enough with that.

'Even the heavens were unruly,' he observed, with his eye to the kaleidoscope. 'The planets wander, you know. Even my mind cannot quite manage the whole universe. But I am glad to have got the world sorted out. Most glad. I shall be all right, now.'

People were returning to the village, unlocking their doors to sniff at the mustiness of cold and neglect, and lighting fires in their dusty grates.

'But it's not the same,' said Toby, mournfully shaking his chins. 'They've seen things they hoped never to know about. They're locking themselves in and keeping themselves to themselves. And who can blame them?'

'We have lost trust in the way the world spins,' said Miss Winter. 'We all know that we must fend for ourselves.' She frowned as a thought struck her. 'You know, we would be more independent if we got ourselves a pig.'

Toby stared at her for a long time. Then he went quite white with shock and amazement.

'A pig?' he echoed. 'But . . . but what about the noise, ma'am? The master has always set his mind against a pig in case of any squealing. It would disturb him, for sure.'

Miss Winter hesitated, but then shrugged.

'The master is disturbed already,' she said, with decision. 'We cannot let his worrying rule our lives. But, on reflection, perhaps *two* pigs might be better;

yes, a boar and a sow, so they can be bred. It would mean feeding them scraps that at the moment go on the compost heaps, but—'

'Pigs,' said Toby, softly, almost reverently. 'Pigs!'

And at once all the sad lines that had pulled down his face for so long curved themselves upwards into an expression of perfect bliss.

They were all kept busy putting things back as they should be. Miss Winter was seized with a maggot for a thorough clean, which was a great annoyance to Rosie: she was sure they'd never get the things dry now that winter was setting in with its characteristic damp determination.

'But I *will* clean away every trace of those men,' said Miss Winter, beating a rug so energetically that the soft fibres parted and tore. 'Oh dear. Oh well, it was never to my taste, in any case. Rosie, you shall polish the boards, instead. We shall soon be ready.'

Ready for what? wondered Will, as he set to work to make good the damage done in the fighting. He sawed wood, and set glue to melt over the brazier, all to the accompaniment of Toby's constant joyful singing, and he watched Mr Gilfry graduate to crutches, and then to a walking stick.

Sam found Miss Winter's old side-saddle hung forgotten in the back of a stall. The surface had dulled, but Sam burnished it up and it went nicely on the flea-bitten grey. After that Miss Winter rode in the paddocks quite often. On bright days you could see her old jacket shining back bravely at the sun.

'Things are getting back in place at last,' she said, one day, clattering back into the courtyard from her ride.

'Yes, ma'am,' said Rosie. 'We have almost everything sorted out, now.'

Miss Winter nodded, and dismounted with a sharp tap of her shoes on the cobbles of the courtyard.

'All in order,' she said. 'Toby with the pigs, and Sam with the horses, and my brother in the tower, and Mrs Keen in the kitchen.'

'Mrs Keen is so happy since she has heard news of Mr Keen,' said Rosie.

'Yes,' said Miss Winter. 'And perhaps they will find a way to be together again. Perhaps that is part of the order of things, too.'

'And so is Will, working in the barn,' said Rosie. 'Or, at least, he would be, if he was in there.'

'But you called me away to mend this clothes prop for you,' protested Will, mildly.

'Yes,' said Miss Winter. 'Everything is ready, here. Everything is in its place, in its pattern, going round and round. But if the country stays quiet then I think I shall try the pattern of a different place. I think I shall go to town. Yes. And I shall take you, Rosie, and perhaps Will, to see us safe.'

Will's heart sank. He had never been to a town, but he doubted very much that it would suit him. But Rosie's eyes were shining with excitement; and, there, he'd have to go along and see what he could make of it, that was all.

'Yes,' said Miss Winter, brightly. 'For, to tell the truth, I am not without hopes of enticing some unwary clerk or attorney into matrimony. Someone useful, with a little money. Unless, of course, I fall in love with a good-for-nothing pauper. But that is a risk one must take.'

'But what of the master, ma'am?' asked Rosie. 'He would not wish to go, for certain.'

But Miss Winter only laughed.

'Oh, he shall not go,' she said. 'Of course he will not go. And why should he, for he does not need me. It was foolish ever to give him a thought, for he never needed me. Not me, myself. And now he has the kaleidoscope, after all.'

Will felt for Rosie's hand.

They were only two pieces of glass, tumbled round, fragile and small, in a wide world. He knew that.

But he closed his eyes to most of it, and he had hope.

Red, for blood. And for soldiers, bright soldiers. Blue. That was for aloneness and sorrow.

Yellow (for gold, for joy); orange (for falling leaves and so for glorious death); purple (for the King, far away, who can kill men with a smile). Green, for rebellion, for hope.

Grey for ignorance. Black for death. White for sickness and the past, ghosts.

All of life, all of life.

Close your eyes . . .

HISTORICAL NOTE

The adventures of William Nunn and his companions take place in the years after the Peterloo Massacre, which occurred in Manchester in 1819. The end of the Napoleonic Wars had led to a rise in unemployment, and this, together with laws designed to keep the price of food high, had caused much hardship. In protest at this, and also at the unfair parliamentary voting system, an open-air meeting was held which attracted as many as 80,000 people. During the meeting soldiers, afraid of a riot or even a rebellion, charged the crowds, causing some deaths and many injuries. As a result of the Massacre the leaders of the crowd were imprisoned, and reform was stifled.

But what, I wondered, would have happened if the Peterloo Massacre *had* led to a large-scale rebellion? Indeed, perhaps in some parallel universe it *did*—and this possibility forms the background to Will's story.

For those readers who wish to know what happened in the end, then I refer them to this short extract from a history of Will's parallel England.

> The site of the Winters' house, which was unfortunately destroyed by Hungarian bombs in 1957, is now completely obliterated, though the road still, of course, remains, as does the public footpath over the downs which was almost certainly used on their return. A Viewing-Point and Tourist Information board are erected close to the place where William Nunn witnessed the beginnings of the bloody and decisive Battle of the Downs.

Census records are tantalizingly incomplete for the period of disruption after the war, but there was certainly a cabinet-maker's shop in the area by 1843, the proprietor of which, one Samuel Holmes Nunn, possesses a surely significant combination of family names, which indicates a substantial rise in the prosperity of the family over the intervening years.

ACKNOWLEDGEMENTS

The writing of this book revealed anew, and with great efficiency, the extraordinary depth and variety of the present author's ignorance. She is pleased to have this opportunity to thank Kath Worrell for making her horse-driving library available on loan, and Jerry Stone FBIS, for explaining so kindly and comprehensibly the, somewhat inconvenient as it turned out, comings and goings of the moon. Information about the use of human dung as a general panacea in the gardens of the times came from the private library of A. J. Ward.

All mistakes, are, however, and of course, the author's very own.

Sally Prue first started making up stories as a teenager, when she realized that designing someone else's adventures was almost as satisfying as having her own. After leaving school Sally joined practically all the rest of her family working at the nearby paper mill. She now teaches recorder and piano and enjoys walking, painting, day-dreaming, reading, and gardening. *Cold Tom*, Sally's first book, won the Bramford Boase Award and the Smarties Prize Silver Award. Sally has two daughters and lives with her husband in Hertfordshire. *Wheels of War* is Sally's eighth novel for Oxford University Press.

ALSO BY SALLY PRUE

THE TRUTH SAYER SEQUENCE

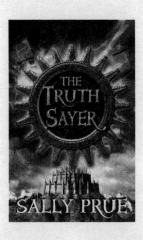

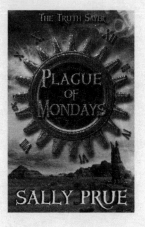

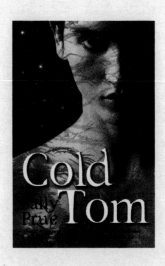

Tom had never been to the city of the demons
before, and it smelt of death. He stood and shivered by
the bridge over the river, his skin prickling with
danger. It was madness to cross—but then he was in
danger if he stayed, too.

Tom is one of the Tribe. But he is not like the
others—he is clumsy and heavy, and the Tribe drive
him away into the demon city. But Tom can't live with
demons either—they are so hot, so foul, and he knows
they are trying to enslave his mind.

But there is nowhere else to run. Between the
savage Tribe and the stifling demons, is there any way
out for Tom?